YOM KIPPUR
IN AMSTERDAM

The Library of Modern Jewish Literature

MAXIM D. SHRAYER

YOM KIPPUR IN AMSTERDAM

Stories

Syracuse University Press

Syracuse University Press
Syracuse, New York 13244-5290
Copyright © 2009 by Maxim D. Shrayer

All Rights Reserved

First Edition 2009

09   10   11   12   13   14   6   5   4   3   2

Individual stories copyright © 1992–2008 by Maxim D. Shrayer

The paper used in this publication meets the minimum requirements
of American National Standard for Information Sciences—Permanence of Paper
for Printed Library Materials, ANSI Z39.48–1992.∞™

For a listing of books published and distributed by Syracuse University Press,
visit our Web site at SyracuseUniversityPress.syr.edu

ISBN-13: 978-0-8156-0918-6

Library of Congress Cataloging-in-Publication Data
Shrayer, Maxim, 1967–
Yom Kippur in Amsterdam : stories / Maxim D. Shrayer. — 1st ed.
p. cm. — (The library of modern Jewish literature)
ISBN 978-0-8156-0918-6 (hardcover : alk. paper)
I. Title.
PG3487.R34Y66 2009
813'.6—dc22
2009017240

Manufactured in the United States of America

To Karen, Mirusha, and Taniusha

MAXIM D. SHRAYER was born in Moscow in 1967 to a Jewish-Russian family. With his parents, the writer and medical scientist David Shrayer-Petrov and the philologist and translator Emilia Shrayer (Polyak), he spent almost nine years as a refusenik. He and his parents left the USSR and immigrated to the United States in 1987, after spending a summer in Austria and Italy.

Shrayer studied at Moscow University, Brown University, Rutgers University, and Yale University, where he received a Ph.D. in 1995. He is professor of Russian and English at Boston College, where he cofounded the Jewish Studies Program. Among Shrayer's books are the critical studies *The World of Nabokov's Stories* and *Russian Poet/Soviet Jew*. A bilingual author and translator, he has published three collections of Russian poetry and edited and cotranslated two books of fiction by his father, David Shrayer-Petrov. Shrayer won a 2007 National Jewish Book Award for his two-volume *Anthology of Jewish-Russian Literature*.

Maxim D. Shrayer is the author of the literary memoir *Waiting for America: A Story of Emigration*. His English-language prose, poetry, and translations have appeared in *Agni, Kenyon Review, Massachusetts Review, Partisan Review, Southwest Review*, and other magazines. He has been the recipient of a number of fellowships, including those from the National Endowment for the Humanities, the Rockefeller Foundation, and the Bogliasco Foundation.

Shrayer lives in Chestnut Hill, Massachusetts, with his wife, Dr. Karen E. Lasser, a medical researcher and physician, and their daughters, Mira Isabella and Tatiana Rebecca.

Yom Kippur in Amsterdam is Shrayer's first collection of stories and first book of fiction.

Contents

Acknowledgments

I AM GRATEFUL to the editors of the periodicals where earlier versions of the stories in this collection appeared.

Versions of three stories in this collection were originally written in Russian: "The Afterlove," "Last August in Biarritz," and "Horse Country." They appeared in Russian as "Staraia rusalka" (*Poberezh'e* 4 [1995]), "Posledniaia liubov' Sokolovitcha" (*Poberezh'e* 6 [1997]), and "Kentavriia" (*Vestnik* [Dec. 15, 1992]); a shorter version of the third story appeared as "Stepnaia strast'" in *Poberezh'e* 7 (1998). In rendering these stories in English, I made structural and atmospheric changes so numerous and so substantial—especially drastic in the case of "The Afterlove," to which I added eight new pages—that the present English texts hardly qualify as "translations" in the conventional sense of the term. The Englished versions were published as "The Afterlove" (*Kenyon Review* 23, nos. 3–4 [2001]), "Last August in Biarritz" (*Agni* 51 [2000]), and "In Horse Country" (*Sí Señor* 2 [2003]).

The remaining five stories were originally composed in English and published as: "The Disappearance of Zalman" (*Sí Señor* 4 [2006]), "Trout Fishing in Virginia" (*Epicenters* 1, no. 1 [2007]), "A Sunday Walk to the Arboretum" (*Epicenters* 2, no. 1 [2008]), "Sonetchka" (*Bee Museum* 1 [2002]), and "Yom Kippur in Amsterdam" (*New Writing* 1, no. 1 [2004]).

I THANK BOSTON COLLEGE for having supported my work over the past thirteen years.

Stephen Vedder and Michael Swanson of Boston College's Media Technology Services once again did a splendid job with the cover.

This book would never have appeared in the present form without the vision and colleagueship of Mary Selden Evans and all my friends at Syracuse University Press. Thank you!

Annie Barva copyedited the manuscript with superb skill, knowledge, tact, and attention to details of exile.

MY FIRST ATTEMPTS at writing fiction in English and at Englishing my Russian-language stories go back to the spring of 1988, when I was the thirteenth, add-on student in the intermediate fiction seminar taught at Brown University by the late John Hawkes. I am grateful to him for having shown attention to a twenty-year-old Jewish kid from Moscow.

At various points, Emily Artinian, Daniel Oliver Bachmann, Graeme Harper, Sean Keck, Thomas Ralph Epstein, Kevin Kopelson, Askold Melnyczuk, Laurence Mintz, Diane Senechal, Christopher Springer, Dabney Stuart, Nancy Zafris, and other colleagues and friends read versions of some or all of these stories. I am thankful for their suggestions and criticisms.

My wife, Karen E. Lasser, and my parents, David Shrayer-Petrov and Emilia Shrayer, took time from their important work to read and comment on drafts of these stories. No words, either in Russian or English, can express my gratitude.

My daughters, Mira Isabella and Tatiana Rebecca, were born during the two years it took this book to assume its final shape. This book is for my wife and my daughters.

M. D. S.

October 2008
Chestnut Hill, Massachusetts

YOM KIPPUR
IN AMSTERDAM

The Disappearance of Zalman

MARK KAGAN MET SARAH at a poetry festival held annually in New Haven. In the packed auditorium their seats were next to each other, but they didn't start talking until the end of the reading. A scandal brought them together—not a scandal in which they took part, but one that both of them observed from their seats. Toward the end of the program, a famous critic was supposed to be reminiscing about Robert Penn Warren and then reciting his poem about goose hunting. Drunk and crab-legged, wearing a wide-brim hat and a soiled corduroy jacket, the professor fell off the stage in the middle of the poem, with the words "path of logic, path of folly" stuck between his teeth.

"This guy's a riot," Sarah said, turning to Mark. "Do you know him?"

"Had him for a seminar," Mark replied, following the curve of her honey-freckled neck, and a few minutes later they were stomping on wet November maple leaves, laughing at each other's impressions of the drunk critic's reading and fall. They headed downtown to Mark's favorite bar and played darts while drinking beer and waiting for their food. After downing a plate of spicy fried squid with two more beers, they walked to Mark's apartment, where the bed hadn't been made and the pillows and sheets smelled of the ocean. . . .

They had been together for a year and a half when Sarah completed her master's in political science and took a job on Capitol Hill. She moved to Washington in August, after the two of them had gone on a biking trip to Prince Edward Island. Mark stayed behind in New Haven to finish up his dissertation and look for a teaching job.

On a wind-flappy, late afternoon in September, Mark was sitting by the window of the bar he frequented. His pint was dark, bitter, and bottomless, the kind that cleanses a drunken soul of its illusions and false hopes. Licking Lethean froth off his lips, his temple pressed to the dusty window between the letters R and A, and his eyes fixated on a neighborhood idiot feeding challah to shameless New Haven pigeons, Mark realized that compromise was just a convenient verbal prop, that of course Sarah wasn't going to become Jewish, or he cease to be it, and they'd better take themselves in hand and face the imminence of separation.

The first few weeks after that were the hardest for Mark. When he wasn't writing, Sarah came into his thoughts, and he revisited their many unresolved discussions about marriage and family. He hoped to find justification for ending the whole thing. Sarah had told him they should let the kids choose their religion. She believed she was meeting him halfway, and a part of him agreed: yes, it looked as if neither one would have to give up their ancestral faith. But when Mark reminded himself that after almost two years together Sarah still hadn't figured out that for a Jewish man the prospect of having to bargain for the identity of his future children was terrifying, he became so angry that he wanted to run away and forget her. As he was soon to discover, though, the rehearsed drama of parting had to play out in his head in order to come to a close in the third act. Only then would it end, when he performed all the parts, including Sarah's, his own, and those of his immigrant parents, Sarah's widowed mother, and even the spectral presence of Sarah's father. Their relationship stubbornly refused to exit the stage, the spectacle of life continued without letting up, Mark kept forgetting their lines and mumbling something about "working it out," coughing and improvising as they went along. It was already the end of October, a feverish Indian summer after a week of cold rain and the first streaks of silver on the ground, but the old double-barreled gun still hadn't shot their love dead.

Mark didn't know how to explain to anyone that despite the certainty of it all, despite his knowledge that his time together with Sarah was nearing its ending, despite the clenched-teeth endorsement of all fifty-seven centuries of Jewish history, he still felt that he would be betraying something so precious that no words could describe it. The Jew in him—the Russian Jew—rejected that which the lover in him still ached for. He was torn; he needed other people's approval. Having concluded that no one, Jew or Gentile, who wasn't equipped to be his perfect double, could justify the decision to break up with Sarah, he resolved to seek a cleric's advice.

It was a foggy morning in early November, almost exactly two years after Mark and Sarah had first met, when Mark went to see the university rabbi. His spacious office, with Chagall's lovers on the walls, was on the third floor of a renovated blue frame house, just steps from the Center for European Art. The rabbi had a barrel chest, short legs, and a clean-shaven face with a hooked nose. He wore a handsomely tailored olive-brown sport coat and sand-colored cords. Sitting in a deep armchair across a glass table from Mark, he listened, chewing the air with his full waxy lips. When Mark finished his story of loving Sarah and trying to leave her, the rabbi took out a pipe, stuffed and lit it, and spoke only after taking a few hungry puffs.

"I think I know how you feel," said the rabbi. "I dated a Catholic girl in college. You must feel like you're in hell, my friend."

"More or less," Mark replied. "More."

"I may as well be direct," the rabbi continued. "You've got two options: either she converts, or you two split up."

Mark sat silently, staring at the rabbi's cognac tassel loafers through the glass table.

"Buy you a cup of coffee?" the rabbi offered, deflating a long pause. He put on a checkered brown derby and wrapped a cashmere scarf around his wiry neck. They went to a nearby bookstore café. One of the block's regular panhandlers greeted them on the way, shaking his paper cup and asking for "a quarter, maybe a buck." The rabbi handed him a crisp dollar bill.

"This guy could be me," the rabbi said under his breath.

Over cappuccino with almond biscotti, the rabbi gave Mark a crash course on conversion and marriage. Unsentimental and prudent, he treated Mark the way an experienced guide treats a testy traveler. Ford the mountain river where I tell you or the swirling waters will swallow you. Don't experiment. Take care! He spoke about the letter of the law. He didn't once mention beauty, desire, longing—all the nimble things that make you love someone or else stop loving her. The rabbi didn't try to persuade Mark. He just laid down his facts and even put some frothy statistics on top. Then he stopped, drank up the last dregs of his cappuccino, and glanced at his wristwatch.

"I have to pick up my daughter from school," he said, getting up.

Mark didn't know what to say.

"Were your parents refuseniks in Russia?" the rabbi asked, leaning over the table.

"Actually, no," Mark replied, feeling guilty for something he hadn't done. "They were rank-and-file engineers. We got permission to leave right away, in '77. I was three; I can barely remember Moscow."

Mark slowly walked home, studying the firmament through the cracks in the asphalt. As he passed the art museum, a voice roused him from a stupor. The voice that said "excuse me" belonged to a tall young man standing on the sidewalk, a stack of yellow leaflets in his left hand. He wore a black coat, black pants, and a white shirt. Wavy blond hair streamed from under his black fedora. Long eyelashes fluttered under his thick glasses like two translucent moths. Thin, reddish vegetation lined his cheeks and upper lip. Something quixotic about him, Mark thought. Now that the young man had Mark's attention, he looked him in the eye and asked: "Are you Jewish?" All the while a myopic smile flickered on his face.

Young men from a local yeshiva showed up on campus about every two months. They parked their rented yellow truck—covered with messianic slogans—on a busy campus street. There they would stand, eyeing and sifting the student crowd, trying to separate the Jew from the chaff. Mark's reactions to these hunters after lost Jewish souls varied from answering "yes" but waving them off with his hand to an occasional visit to the yellow truck, where he repeated a vaguely familiar prayer after one of the yeshiva boys. And that November afternoon he followed the young man from another century inside the yellow truck.

"Mark Kagan," he introduced himself.

The young man smiled and offered him a hand with long fingers that were made to caress a musical instrument.

"I'm Zalman, Zalman Kun."

"Are you related to the Hungarian revolutionary?" Mark asked.

"My grandfather came from Hungary. How do you know about *that* Kun?"

"Jewish trivia."

After Zalman had released Mark from a double harness of phylacteries, he put his hand on Mark's wrist.

"Tell me, do you know Hebrew?"

"Barely," Mark answered retreating toward the back of the truck. "Sunday school was a total disaster."

"What about now?"

"I've tried. Don't have the patience. In any case, I should be going." Mark shook the young Hasid's hand and turned to exit.

"Wait," Zalman sang out. "You know, you can come to my yeshiva and learn Hebrew. If you want, I can be your tutor. Free of charge."

From his chest pocket he removed a yellow flyer with a picture of a smiling old man with a round beard. Folding the flyer in half, he scribbled a phone number on it and placed it in Mark's hand.

Two days later, under the influence of some fatidic gravity, Mark found himself turning his old Subaru wagon into a side street and driving up to Zalman's yeshiva. The yeshiva was about a mile west of the university campus, and Mark had never been to that part of town before. Neon signs offered to cash his checks, to sell him liquor or barbecued wings and ribs. Parking outside the yeshiva, he felt like a traveler nearing an Israelite enclave amid the land of Egyptians.

Three skinny boys in velvet yarmulkes stood on the front steps of a yellow Victorian. Their faces looked phosphorescent in the streetlamp's light.

"Who're you looking for?" asked one of them, a kid with circles under squirrel eyes.

"Zalman, he's one of the students here," Mark replied.

"Zalman?"

With both hands the boy pulled at the ornate knob of the heavy front door and led Mark to a room with dark wood paneling. Young men in black-and-white garb were sitting at the tables, bent over their books. Several of them were swaying and burbling some words.

Zalman saw Mark and got up to shake his hand. "You came for your first lesson, that's very good."

He put his hand on the little kid's shoulder and said something to him in Yiddish. The kid giggled and ran out of the study hall.

Zalman pointed to a chair. "Sit down. Please. I have a little practice book for you."

Mark sat down across the table from Zalman. Opening a yellow booklet with the Hebrew alphabet on the last page, Zalman put his index finger next to a character.

"What's this?" he asked.

"Gimmel," Mark answered.

"And this?"

"Kof. No, Chof."

"Very good," Zalman said, stressing the "very" part. "*Very* good. And what's this?"

"Hmm . . . either Vov or Zayen. I always get them confused. Both look like little cripplets."

Zalman sighed and laid out his aristocratic hands on the table.

"I want you to know the entire alphabet next time." He closed the yellow booklet and passed it to Mark. "And now let me ask you a question."

"You probably think I'm hopeless."

"No, no, no. I just wanted to ask you what sort of things you learn at your university." Zalman said "learn" instead of "study."

"I study literature."

"Literature?" Zalman repeated, tasting the word with his lips and tongue.

"I'm writing a dissertation about modern Jewish writers who wrote in European languages. That's basically my area."

"Why do you call them *Jewish* writers?"

"They were Jews, and many of them wrote about Jews."

"Did they write good or bad things about Jewish people?"

"It's not as simple as that. Some good, some bad."

"I understand," said Zalman, in whose gray eyes centuries of sorrow were now reflected.

"Haven't you read any books by Jewish writers?" Mark asked. "Kafka? Joseph Roth? Malamud? Philip Roth?"

"Roth? I've heard about him. He wrote bad things about Jewish people."

"Not bad. Sometimes brutally honest."

"We have our own stories. Beautiful." Zalman lifted up a stack of volumes in crimson bindings.

It was raining when Mark left the yeshiva. He lit a cigarette and stood on the porch for a while, inhaling tobacco smoke and the rotten breath of Long Island Sound.

DURING THAT WHOLE AUTUMN Sarah came to see Mark in New Haven only twice. She usually had to work on Saturdays. As the one with a flexible schedule—those were Sarah's words—Mark would drive or take the train to Washington on many weekends. Instead of the dissertation he was trying to finish, he could have written one about the exalted sense of expectation, the railroad conspiracies, the devilish traffic jams and sardonic state troopers, and the late Friday night arrivals when he and Sarah both pattered in the car like impatient children.

Unfinished conversations thrived amid such weekends of packing a life without each other into thirty-six hours. Saturdays often ended dissonantly as Mark and Sarah were cross with each other for having to part the next day. They would sleep late on Sunday, read the paper, and hurry to brunch. On Monday, when Mark woke up alone in his own bed, the sinewy calendar would wink at him from a half-open door. Add to that two more chapters to go in his dissertation and the bleakness of the job market, and the story of his last autumn in graduate school would be near complete (save for the vertiginous transparency of the New England sky on a crisp December morning, which words refuse to capture).

Without Sarah his life would have been all work laced with brooding and procrastination. But in this life a niche had been carved out for his tutor, Zalman, whom Mark went to see at the yeshiva on Wednesday nights. He didn't make much progress in Hebrew. Zalman turned out to be a great storyteller, and instead of tutoring Mark in language, he told him wondrous tales about tzaddiks from Galicia and Volhynia who in their sleep visited with the Almighty. Mark, in turn, would retell his favorite short stories or even summarize entire novels. "Levin, that's a Jewish name!" Zalman cried out when they got to *Anna Karenina*, and happiness glinted in his gray eyes. . . .

Sarah hadn't been to New Haven since Labor Day weekend. She finally visited in December, arriving by plane on a Friday night. In the small and shabby terminal, her navy raincoat, pinstripe suit, firebird scarf, and pearls clashed with Mark's faded jeans and old suede jacket.

"Hey, yeshiva boy," she said, clinging to him and kissing him on a scruffy cheek. She said it almost too loudly and merrily, and several passengers from Sarah's flight looked at them over their shoulders. Mark cringed, just slightly, at the new nickname Sarah had for him. She used to call him "Russian boy," and he wasn't crazy about that nickname either. He didn't think of himself as "Russian," although he still spoke some Russian with his parents and poured white vinegar over the meat dumplings he bought frozen at the Russian store when he visited his parents in Boston—and cooked for himself at home.

"I'd like to shower and change before we eat," Sarah said as they were pulling out of the airport, her hand climbing over the collar of his shirt. "I've missed you, yeshiva boy. How's the diss?"

Mark drove silently, whistling and pretending that he didn't want to talk about his dissertation. He didn't want to talk about anything at all.

"How's the congressman?" he finally asked about Sarah's boss.

"He's good. He had to go to Oakland this weekend for his nephew's christening."

Sarah's lacy, bottle green underwear made her look taller and slenderer in the bedroom's semidarkness. As she undressed, Mark was thinking that his desire for her had become a separate creature living outside his mind. Afterward, their bodies disentangled, they lay on his futon, smoking and touching the rims of each other hands. Purple dusk draped the windows from the outside. Upstairs, Mark's Brazilian neighbor was playing something jazzy and tropical—unwinding after her long shift at the city hospital. Mark turned on the bedside lamp, and they looked at the pictures from their summer vacation, which he had finally developed six months later.

"So, how's the yeshiva?" Sarah asked.

"It's good."

"What do you talk about, you and your tutor?"

"Many things. Judaism. Death."

"Do you talk about women?"

"Not really."

"Never?"

"I guess we do," Mark replied hesitantly. "We talk about marriage. And he tells stories."

"Stories? What about?"

"This week he told me about this rabbi whose wife died. But then she visited him every year on a hot July night and took him for a stroll around the small town. The rabbi's second wife was growing mad with jealousy."

"Doesn't your tutor ask after me?"

"He knows you exist."

"Interesting," Sarah drew out. "I just can't picture you going there."

"Well, I can picture you going to mass," he snapped.

A couple of weeks earlier Mark had mentioned to Zalman that he was driving to Washington for the weekend.

"Why are you going?" Zalman asked.

"To see my girlfriend."

"Girlfriend? What's her name?"

"Sarah."

"Sarah—that's nice. And what does she do?"

With a few strokes of embellishment Mark created a Jewish version of Sarah Flaherty. She and Mark had met in graduate school. Her family lived in California. Her father was an ophthalmologist, her mother a social worker. (Before his death of liver cirrhosis, Sarah's father had operated a truck-leasing company in Sacramento; her mother still worked as a bank teller.) She played the cello (at college the Catholic Sarah had sung in an a capella group). The Jewish Sarah was working as a legislative assistant to a senator from San Francisco (the real Sarah actually worked for a congressman from Bakersfield). She had long copper hair and turquoise blue eyes (she did!). Zalman nodded in satisfaction as Mark described this other Sarah.

Lying next to the real Sarah, Mark felt doubly the liar as he tried to ward off her questions about Zalman and the yeshiva. Sarah was the only thing he wasn't truthful about with Zalman, that and the fact of his Russian—Soviet—origins.

"I want to meet this Zalman character," Sarah said and got out of bed.

"Why?" Mark asked, feeling cornered.

"I just want to. Let's invite him to have dinner with us tonight," Sarah said, putting on Mark's striped terry robe.

"Sarah, it's Shabbat. I can't even call him until tomorrow night."

"What about brunch or coffee Sunday morning?"

"Aren't you going to mass?"

"You know I don't go every Sunday," Sarah replied, lips pursing.

"Okay then, what do you want me to do?" Mark asked.

"Call him."

"Zalman?"

"Yes, Zalman, the famous Zalman. Call him tomorrow night and have him meet us Sunday morning."

"What if he's busy or something?"

"Dear heart, this is getting ridiculous. Just tell the guy we want to invite him to brunch. I'm going to take a shower now."

Sunday morning they ended up meeting Zalman at the bookstore café where Mark had gone with the rabbi. The place was crowded with the regulars, noses and chins stuck to their Sunday papers. Mark glanced across the café's two vaulted sections, recognizing a female couple from comp lit and a corpulent professor of Italian with a glistening head. Mark avoided Sarah's searching eyes while they stood waiting for a table to free up.

Zalman flew into the café as Mark and Sarah were hanging their jackets on the velour chair backs. The broad collar of Zalman's white shirt hovered above his coat's shiny lapels. He was flushed; a deep red splotch covered not only his cheeks but the whole length of his ordinarily pale face.

"I'm late, I'm sorry," he said addressing an invisible third person sitting somewhere between Mark and Sarah. "I borrowed my friend Aron's car, and it wouldn't start. Ooph!"

"It's nice to meet you, Zalman," Sarah said, putting out her hand. "Sorry we roused you from your studies."

Zalman dithered but then timidly shook Sarah's hand, holding it like a cello bow.

"Whachya havin', Zalman?" Mark asked, trying to sound crass. "Our treat."

"I think I'll have a cup of tea."

"Just tea?" Sarah put in a question. "What about an omelet—they have great—"

"—Sarah," Mark interrupted. "Unlike myself, Zalman keeps kosher."

"That's okay," Zalman said. "I had a big breakfast. Tea will be fine."

The waiter brought their teas and coffees—Zalman's came in a paper cup. There was silence while they ripped their packs of sugar and stirred the contents of their mugs.

"So Zalman," Sarah said. "Mark tells me you're a great storyteller."

"That's nice of him," Zalman replied.

"He actually described to me the story you told this week. The one about a rabbi and his dead wife that came to visit. It sounds like so much fun."

"We have wonderful stories."

"Well, curious gal that I am, I have a question for you."

"Yes?"

"It's connected to the story you told Mark. Sort of."

"Please ask," Zalman said, moving forward in his chair.

"Where do you think we go when we die?"

Sarah's question made Mark spill coffee on the table.

"Good question," Zalman said. "Great Jewish thinkers used to argue about this."

"But what do you think?"

"I think when we die, we go off to a beautiful place, more beautiful than you or Mark or I or anyone else can ever imagine."

"And there?" Sarah pressed on. "What happens there?"

"And there we're joined with our loved ones for eternity. Not we, our souls. There is no time there, no time and no space."

Feeling increasingly annoyed with Sarah's questions and Zalman's princely patience, Mark decided to take the bait.

"Excuse me," he interceded. "Why did the dead wife visit her husband, then?"

"What do you mean?" said Zalman and looked at him in bewilderment.

"I mean, why couldn't she wait for him in that place where she was?"

"She probably missed him," Sarah said, smiling innocently. "She probably couldn't wait to see him."

Zalman's fingers began to twitch. "Well—"

"First of all, if there's no time in the other world, souls who are already there cannot miss anything or anyone, can they?" Mark fired off, suddenly proud of the Talmudic blood pulsating in his veins.

"Maybe," Zalman conceded.

"If that much is true, I can see why the living husband would miss his dead wife, but not the other way around."

"My friends," Zalman said, turning his face first to Sarah, then to Mark, "you must understand a couple of things. First, about marriage. A divine bond exists between a wife and a husband. Do you understand?"

"Of course I do," Sarah replied in a Girl Scout's ringing voice.

Mark didn't say anything.

"And also," Zalman continued, "I want to tell you something about the world to come. There are no bodies there. Just pure spirit.

And since there are no bodies, we experience no desires in that world. And no jealousy."

Zalman unclasped his hands and opened his fingers as if he were letting out a dove.

"These are complicated questions," he concluded.

In silence they waited for the check. Then, turning the empty paper cup in his slender hands, Zalman addressed Mark.

"When are you and Sarah getting married?"

"Oh, I don't know, one day," Mark said, clearing his throat. "Right now we're both too busy to start a family."

"A Jew should never be too busy to have a family."

"So how come you aren't married?" Mark asked.

"I will be. Soon."

"When? Who is she?" Sarah asked eagerly.

"I don't know yet. But I know she will be great." A dreamy smile illumined Zalman's face.

"And how will you meet her?" Sarah asked again. Turning to her, Mark discovered that her eyes were filled with strange glee.

"Sarah, please," Mark tried to stop her, but Zalman placed his hand over Mark's wrist, indicating that he didn't mind being interrogated.

"All I can tell you," Zalman answered, "is that it will happen soon. I just know it will."

Giggling, Sarah straightened her silk scarf.

Outside, having said their good-byes to Zalman, they stood on the sidewalk, taking in the dainty sunlight. Zalman got into a saggy brown Buick with corroded bumpers and drove off.

"He's very passionate about his faith," Sarah said.

"That's his whole life."

"Interesting."

"What's interesting?" Mark asked.

"I'd never met such a spiritual Jew before. I can see why you'd be in awe of him."

"You do?"

They spent the afternoon bumbling in and out of stores on Chapel Street and ended up buying only fancy note paper and a couple of other trifles for Sarah. They ate calzones and Greek salad at the place they used to go to when Sarah still lived in town. After taking Sarah to the airport, Mark drove straight to his bar and sat there until closing. He watched basketball, sipping porter and mulling over their brunch with Zalman and Sarah's excitement—so unforeseen.

IN THE MIDDLE OF JANUARY Zalman told Mark he was leaving New Haven. The Rebbe, he said, was sending him to Washington to teach at one of the centers there. For a year. And then to South America. He promised to stay in touch. He passed Mark on to another tutor, Aron, a Jewish giant with red, meaty cheeks and enormous arms and legs. The new tutor tried to assign written homework. He didn't tell stories and smiled viciously at Mark's errors. Mark stopped going to the yeshiva.

Two months later he finally heard from Zalman—on a late afternoon in March during a snowstorm. Mark was sitting at his desk, sipping tea with milk and proofreading the final chapter of his dissertation.

"Mark? This is Zalman, from the yeshiva. You remember me?"

"Zalman, where on earth are you? I had no way of getting in touch with you!"

"I'm in Washington. Things have been very, very busy. How are you, Mark?"

"I'm okay. My dissertation's due next week."

"Your what?"

"My dissertation, my thesis." There was a lot of static on the line, so Mark had to scream.

"And how's your girlfriend?"

"She's fine."

"Still in Washington?"

"Yep, still working for her congressman."

"You said she worked for a senator," Zalman said.

"Senator, congressman . . . it's all the same," Mark replied.

"What do you mean?"

"Things are actually on the rocks between us."

"Why?" Zalman's voice dropped.

"It's a long story."

"Fine, some other time you'll tell me."

"Are you coming to the yeshiva anytime soon?" Mark asked after a short pause.

"I don't know. Maybe in summer."

"I may not be here in summer."

Zalman also said something in Yiddish—probably to someone standing next to him. "Mark, I have to go. I'll call you next week," he said and hung up.

Mark wasn't at all surprised when the following week passed, then the one after it, and Zalman still hadn't called. He felt like a character in one of Zalman's tales of death and desire.

IT WASN'T UNTIL the middle of June that Mark received another call from Zalman Kun. Puffy rain clouds were standing guard over New Haven. It had been a chilly morning. Mark had taken his daily stroll around the grounds of the theological seminary where graduate students and old-timers walked their dogs. He didn't have a dog to walk—he only had a pet tortoise named Hèloîse who roamed about his apartment and ate cabbage and carrot peel. But he liked to watch dogs at play and even got to know a few owners over the five years he had lived in the same apartment on Whitney Avenue. Mark had come back from the walk and looked around his living room, overflowing with boxes and crates and stacks of folders on the floor.

He had decided to make some tea, read the paper, and then continue with the packing.

Earlier that morning Mark hadn't gotten very far at packing up his belongings. It seemed as though his telephone had just been connected and everyone in the world had decided to call him at once. First, his grandfather's younger brother, Miron, telephoned to congratulate him on his Ph.D. Then his cousin Marina had phoned from New York to tell him about a Jewish medical resident from South Africa she had "met on the net." Of course, his parents had called, each of them separately, as they always did in the morning. And then his college roommate Alec Ziolkowski, a naval intelligence officer, had phoned to tell Mark of his promotion to lieutenant-commander.

Mark was in the kitchen fixing himself a tongue sandwich when the phone rang again.

"It's Zalman."

"Where are you, Zalman?"

"Brooklyn. I'll be here for two weeks. How are you, Mark?"

"Let's see . . . I defended my diss, and I'm moving to Maine—I got a job at a small college there."

"A real professor," Zalman said weightily. "That's wonderful. Mazel tov!"

"What's going on with you?" Mark asked.

"Things are very good, Boruch Hashem," Zalman answered. Mark heard children screaming in the background. "Mark? Can I call you later? Maybe tomorrow? Or the day after?"

"Sure, Zalman. I'm here for another week."

"Bye. *Zai gezunt*," Zalman said and hung up.

That night Mark had a dream about a wedding—Zalman's wedding. When Zalman's bride opened her veil before joining him under the chuppah, he saw a familiar freckled face, full lips, luminous eyes. In the dream Mark saw himself and Zalman dancing in a circle of jubilant Jews in black and white—saw Zalman's light frame, wavy blonde hair, saintly smile. The eyes of a man who strides with the angels.

Zalman never called him again. A year later Mark learned from a mutual friend that Sarah Flaherty had married a Jew and moved with him to Argentina.

Trout Fishing in Virginia

AT THIRTY-NINE, Andrew Lance was the nation's youngest poet-laureate. He told reporters and public-radio hosts that he was working on a novel in verse about a middle-aged American man who felt like a samurai in a world of crumbling principles and decaying honor. "He's done well for himself writing odes to rusting steel mills," grumbled fellow poets who had known Lance back when he used to take summer courses at the famous writing school in the Green Mountains. They were certainly right that he had done better than most of them—an Ivy League professorship ("IV League," Lance liked to tell his students, stressing the "vee" part and thus the age of his esteemed colleagues); a Pulitzer plus a necklace of other prizes and awards; a Colonial on the Main Line and a summer cottage on Block Island; a Boticellian wife and two children—and all achieved through rhyme and reason.

His peers were still teaching a writing course here, a seminar there, freelancing and even ghost writing, and still sending out work with the nauseating self-addressed stamped envelopes, whereas he now edited one of the nation's oldest quarterlies, occasionally publishing an old friend, but preferring to feature new names. The more or less established *littérateurs*, whom Lance had once known and later refused to print, spoke of his patronage of younger writers, especially female ones, as something political and therefore disingenuous—a pose. These jealous poets couldn't fathom that in discovered authors lay for Lance the promise of a new life—enchanting, angular, winged.

This hunt for new talent had grown into an obsession since Lance had been named poet-laureate. About once a month he traveled to a university campus to give a reading and meet the students in the creative writing program. A creature of routine, he liked to arrive on a Thursday, spend a few hours with students, in the evening give a reading followed by a book signing, and get home by midday or afternoon on Friday. From his trips Lance returned with a booty—a batch of poems and stories to read during the week. Weekends belonged to his family: his wife, Jill, an attorney with an old Philadelphia firm, who cooked Asian fusion on Saturdays; his thirteen-year-old son, Elton, crazy about sailing and about Japanese, which he was taking at his private school; and his eleven-year-old daughter—raven-curled, dreamy Annabel, who had taken after the Lance side of the family. (Their name used to be Lansky, and in her occasional moments of jolliness Jill referred to her husband's family as "the gangsters.") Annabel composed rhymed poems and showed them to her father on weekends. Their ritual.

On a tepid Thursday afternoon two weeks before Thanksgiving, Lance got off the plane at Dulles and headed to the car rental counter. He never checked luggage—he distrusted the aircraft's womb. He also didn't like limos or drivers with their wrinkled cheap tuxedos, their lurid tales, and their rancid breath. He enjoyed the sensation of driving alone through this vast country, which still enveloped and comforted the traveler as she had once opened herself to his grandparents and three-year-old father after their flight from Podolia in 1920.

Andrew Lance was tall and bony, with thick black brows, a long chin, and a Caesar cut. He was wearing brown cords with a silverish sheen, an olive shirt and a navy sweater, a coat of very soft suede, and matching suede loafers. Although his picture had been printed in many newspapers and news magazines, no one recognized Lance on the plane or later in the airport's afternoon crowd. He carried a beige garment bag over his shoulder, and in his hands he held a leather briefcase with gilded buckles and an aluminum tube covered in green canvas. The tube was a travel case; it contained his new fly-fishing rod. His wife had given him the rod for their fifteenth anniversary—an expensive present, an exquisite one to those who knew about fly-fishing. The rod had been made by hand in Stevens Point, Wisconsin, his initials embroidered on the case and engraved on a copper plate; Lance intended to test it during the trip. He hadn't brought chest waders this time, having packed only hiking boots, his vest, and his fly-fishing hat. On the Web, he had researched the area around the campus where he was heading and had found a state park with accessible trout streams and a place to buy a permit during the weekend.

THIS NOVEMBER VISIT was unusual in two respects. As a rule Lance avoided reading at well-known colleges and universities, preferring instead the lesser, sometimes outright obscure campuses. He was especially reluctant to appear at universities with strong writing programs and extended faculties of poets, fictionists, and playwrights. He acknowledged to himself that his was a kind of reverse snobbism—the more provincial the school, the more promise it would hold for him. This time, however, he had agreed to speak at an old southern university with a well-respected MFA program—mainly because Jeremiah McCloy, a friend from college, taught poetry there. McCloy was a native Virginian, a minister's son. Even as a freshman at Dartmouth, McCloy had been ruddy and heavyset, a bit sedate. In his adulthood, he was Lance's opposite in everything, from his passion for bird-watching to the cherry pipe he suckled even when it wasn't lit. McCloy wrote cavernous, uninspiring, meticulously researched nature poems about Virginia's shales and granites and toothlike roots and gumlike newts, and Lance admired them, though he didn't even know why. Perhaps because he himself could never write something so close to soil and verity.

And so Lance agreed to read at his friend's university and even to stay an extra day. He planned to give a reading Thursday night, spend time with McCloy and his students on Friday, get up early on Saturday, fish for a few hours, and then drive straight to the airport. On clear days toward the middle of November, Lance knew, trout feed with abandon.

It took him more than two hours to reach the southern corner of the Shenandoah Valley. He drove on back roads, taking his time, tasting under his tongue the smells of resting earth, of hay and manure, taking in the landscape with its silos, rolling hills, and bobbing forms of farmers. He stopped at a rural luncheonette and ordered country-fried chicken steak, beans, mashed yams. "Hun, would you like sweet iced tea?" the waitress asked him. While waiting for his food and sipping iced tea that felt sour on the gums, Lance talked to a couple of farmers—also sitting at the counter—about the weather forecast for the weekend and about local fishing. They had heard of the place where he wanted to fish, still an hour away from where he stopped, but had never been "down by the university." They said they fished for bass and catfish, never trout. "You a professor or something?" asked one of the farmers, a stocky fellow with pale brown skin and eyes set close together. Lance smiled. "Something like that," he said. The conversation died, and a few minutes later the farmers finished their coffees, carefully wiped their mouths and fingers, and left.

The campus, its oldest section built in the 1800s, was in a richer part of town. Driving through this area on the way to his lodge, Lance saw groomed homes with wraparound porches and wide front and back lawns. The university had offered to put him up at a downtown hotel, but he had asked to stay near the campus instead. There was a university guest house, an old mansion, he had been told, but Lance knew it could mean a trap—uninvited admirers. The motor lodge on the edge of the campus was called Virginia Arms. Lance brought in his things, washed up, and then dialed his friend

McCloy's number. They agreed that Lance would walk over to McCloy's office and the two of them would spend some time alone before joining deans and members of the English department for an official dinner. The dinner was at six; the reading was scheduled for eight at the university theater.

Lance showered, then lay naked under the sheets with his eyes closed, thinking of the dinner and the provincial pleasantries he would have to endure. He dozed off for a bit and woke up rested—something he had learned as a teenager from his father, who always took a short nap after coming home from his pharmacy. Lance got up, brushed his teeth, put on a French blue shirt, black slacks of weightless summer wool, and a gray blazer, and studied himself in the mirror. In his briefcase was his new collection of verse, from which he intended to read. It was a little chilly without a coat, but he didn't want to turn back—a bad omen in his anthology of superstitions. Following a campus map that his friend had left for him at the reception desk, the way to McCloy's office marked in purple ink, Lance stopped in the shadow of a great sycamore to read a memorial plaque attached to a white stone pillar. The plaque, or actually a wreath of cast iron with a sign inside it, marked the grave of a general's horse; he chuckled as he pulled out a small leather-bound notebook with a slender gold pencil and copied down the text: "Here lies Hannibal, the beloved horse. . . . "

Lance had last seen Jeremiah McCloy a year and a half ago, at the funeral of A. D. Milch, their former mentor in whose poetry seminar at Dartmouth they had befriended each other almost twenty years earlier. McCloy's office smelled of pipe tobacco and something else, something musky. To a stranger, the room would have suggested, with all the objects on its shelves and walls, that its occupant taught geology or botany. Reclining in a big chair, Lance remembered seeing his friend for the first time when they were nineteen and green. Now showing a spiderweb of wrinkles on his rubicund face, a pot-belly . . . but otherwise the same southern boy with a twinkling smile and a rich and slightly archaic vocabulary. McCloy brought two cups of coffee from a kitchenette down the hall from his office. He settled into his chair and rested his mug on his right knee.

"So, Andy," asked McCloy. "How's fame?"

"Fame's good. She's also transient," Lance laughed. "You're next, Jerry."

"I don't think so. You know my stuff. Minerals. Grasses. It's tedious to most people."

"Your stuff is absolutely yours," Lance replied with passion. "By the way, did you get the proofs?" (Lance was publishing McCloy's long poem about a great-uncle's funeral in Roanoke.)

"I did, they look clean. Just a couple of typos. Thank you, Andy. You know you didn't have to do it."

"I wanted to."

They chatted about two poets they both had known in college, who had recently published new books. Then they turned to the topic of families—both had married in their midtwenties and now had teenage children.

"Have you been in touch with Lydia?" McCloy asked.

"You know, in the last years before his death there wasn't much love lost between me and old Milch."

"I believe I knew that," said McCloy. "Lydia's been having a hard time. I telephone her about twice a month."

Lydia Gershteyn, a translator of Spanish and Latin American poets, was A. D. Milch's widow. She and A. D. Milch had met in Spain. Lydia had been very kind to Lance and McCloy when they were her husband's poetry students at Dartmouth. Gripped by a pang of guilt, Lance recalled the last time he and Milch had spoken. That year's Pulitzers had just been announced, and Lance had been on national television for the first time. Milch had called him that evening. Things had been tense between them for a while and tenser since Lance had assumed the editorship of his quarterly. Lance had known things would explode sooner or later.

"I saw you on television," Milch had said in his bellowing voice.

"How are you, Axel?"

"Don't give me that cordial crap, Lance. You know why I'm calling."

"To tell me I don't deserve it."

"Back in the 1930s people like you used to write touchy-feely poems about the Spanish Civil War instead of going there and fighting Franco."

"Not everyone is as brave as you."

"Don't placate me. I still remember you as a kid from a midwestern suburb."

"That makes two of you," Lance tried to joke it off. "You and my mother."

"You know what your problem is, Lance?"

"Fine, Axel, tell me what my problem is."

"It's not that you lack skill, Lance. It's that you're just too bourgeois, too damn bourgeois to be an American poet."

Milch had slammed down the phone, and Lance had stood there clutching the receiver, unable to shake off his mentor's wrath. "Bourgeois, too damn bourgeois," he had chewed on Milch's words while going back in his mind to his parents' Colonial in Cleveland Heights, to his mother's temple sisterhood. . . .

McCloy's breezy voice brought Lance back from his recollection. "Andy, we should probably get going. It's almost six."

"Okay."

"The old man was jealous of you," McCloy said, smiling at Lance.

"I don't know, Jerry. I don't know who was jealous of whom."

They walked to McCloy's Jeep and drove in silence. The dinner in Lance's honor was being held in the candle-lit dining room of a renovated country inn. Logs were burning in a large fireplace near the far end of a long table. About twenty guests were already sitting along its sides. A few people applauded when Lance and McCloy entered. Smiling at no one in particular, Lance looked around the room. On the walls there were antlers and a boar's head, framed hunting scenes, and old maps. After a walk round the table, during which McCloy patiently introduced him to those gathered in his honor, Lance was seated in the middle of the table between a bald man with a ferocious beard and huge arms and a petite woman with matte white skin and a low-cut silk blouse. The man was the local eminence Robinson Dilliard; the woman his wife, Mary-Adaire, a watercolorist, as Lance soon found out. Lance vaguely recalled reading a story by Dilliard in an anthology of southern writers that he had picked up at a used-book shop in Cleveland while visiting his mother. In addition to countless stories and eight or nine novels, Dillard had to his credit a book about ghosts in Vladimir Nabokov's fiction. The book had come out in the late 1960s, and Nabokov had promptly demolished it in an interview. Ever since then Dilliard had worn Nabokov's comment as a venomous badge of courage; no new acquaintance, Lance included, was spared a long retelling of the incident. Squeezed between Dilliard and his perfumed wife ("You must try the breast of duck with cognac reduction," she chortled into Lance's ear), Lance hardly spoke with any of the other guests during the dinner.

The university theater was packed, people even standing in the back and a few students sitting on the steps in the aisles. As a rule, Lance never said anything before reading his poetry. This time, because he had overdosed on southern hospitality and because he liked what his friend McCloy had said in his introduction, he decided to start with opening remarks. He came out to the podium, a bottle of water in one hand, a volume of his poems in another.

"Professor McCloy has shared with you one of the many maxims of our late teacher," Lance began. "Axel Milch—you probably know him as A. D. Milch—passed away less than two years ago. When Jerry and I started college, Axel Milch meant the world to both of us and our other classmates. He knew everything about poetry. I confess, Axel and I didn't exactly see eye to eye during the latter years of his life, but being here on your campus, around you, and spending time with my friend Jerry, I'm inspired to remember Axel Milch and to share with you one of the things he told us about writing verse. You've got to bleed over your poems. You've got to write each poem thinking you may die tomorrow, and this is your last one, and the world will judge you based on this one poem."

Lance raised his dark eyebrows, as though signaling to the audience that he himself wasn't sure what to make of his teacher's words.

"I try to do that in my own work," he added. "It doesn't always happen."

Lance took a long sip of water and put the bottle down. He read for about thirty minutes in his humid voice with short consonants. Then he stepped down from the stage to a table with a display of his books and a blonde girl from the bookstore who blushed when he sat beside her to sign books. Lance liked the signing part because he got to see the actual human beings who bought his books and took them home. During signings he was at his most charming, lifting the guard that he kept on while on stage. As Lance smiled absently at a line of southern college students and local ladies waiting for his autograph, he thought about going back to his room at Virginia Arms, about having a drink of Scotch from a silver flask that, like his elegant fishing rod, was a present from his wife, about the meeting with McCloy's students scheduled for the following day, and about the trout fishing that would crown the visit.

He must have signed forty copies that evening; his hand ached from writing variations of the same words. He took the last sip of his water, put away his own marked-up copy with a black leather bookmark and closed the cap of his luxurious fountain pen. He waved to McCloy who was sitting in the front row and waiting to take him home.

"Good reading, Andy," said McCloy. "Whenever you're ready."

Lance was shaking the hand of the girl from the bookstore when a woman with long, loose hair walked up the aisle to the table with his books. She wore a long skirt of crinkled lavender material and a faded blue denim jacket. Dangling on her right shoulder was a bag made of embroidered sackcloth.

"Professor Lance, would you sign my copy?" she asked.

"I'd be delighted," Lance replied, reaching his left hand across the table to take the copy from the woman's hands and removing his pen from his chest pocket with his right. Then both his hands stopped in flight as he stared at the woman's face, arrested in the moment of recognition.

"Tammy? Tammy LaGrange?"

"Hello, Drew. It's nice to see you," she said. She spoke with an old Virginian accent.

"Good God, Tammy! What are you doing here?" said Lance, his mouth drying up.

"I live here. It's been a long time, Drew, hasn't it?"

"Let me see . . . sixteen, seventeen years?"

"Something like that," Tammy tilted her head and smiled. "Fame becomes you, Drew. And I very much liked the poems you read. I knew some already."

Lance walked around the table and stood next to the woman. He was stroking his thumbs with his index fingers—something he did when agitated.

"Tammy, this is so unexpected, it's great to see you. My friend's waiting . . . I'd like to talk and catch up when I'm not in a rush . . . It would be ridiculous to have been here and . . . What are you doing for supper tomorrow?"

"I have two kids and a husband. Normally we go out Friday night, but I might be able to get a night off." She smiled again, and Lance remembered kissing her dimples many years ago under the summer night sky of Vermont.

"That would be nice," said Lance.

"Where're you staying?"

"Virginia Arms," he answered with a restless laugh. "Room 117."

"So why don't we say I'll call you in the afternoon, about three."

"What's your phone number, just in case?"

"I'll call you, Drew. Bye."

She walked toward the exit, her hips swaying with a graceful laziness. Lance saw that she was wearing brown cowboy boots.

"Meet an old friend?" McCloy asked Lance after he started the engine.

"Believe it or not—here of all places. She used to write great stuff. Jerry, I think I might meet her for dinner tomorrow. I hope it's okay with you and Molly."

"Oh, fine. Maybe afterwards you'll stop by for a piece of pie with ice cream."

"Sure you don't mind my breaking our plans?"

McCloy nodded and kept silent while driving Lance back to his lodge.

Lance's first impulse was to call his wife. But the impulse disappeared like concentric circles spreading out from an angler's float dropped on the water's surface. Lance took off his clothes and hung them slowly and neatly. Wearing only boxers and a white T-shirt, he sat in front of the TV set. For a few minutes he flipped the channels mindlessly; then he got up and poured himself a drink from his flask. The Scotch burned his palate; it tasted of resin. Like a silver nebula, the image of Tammy LaGrange pulsed in his head. She had put on a little weight, and her face had a shininess that illumined the beginnings of a second chin. Her dress and manner were earthy, but not in the artful way of English department granolas, Lance noted. She's this, she's that, he mocked himself. She was still every breath as seductive, alluring, as she once was.

Lance stood under the shower, stooping because the shower head was too low. The towels were small and flimsy, and he got under the

sheets feeling wetness on his chest and groin. He turned off the bedside lamp and closed his eyes; his eyelids felt hot and itchy, too small
to cover his eyes. He lay awake on his back for a long time, unable
to sleep. He lost track of time. A flood of memories rocked him as
it carried him back to the old campus that lay, like a platter of New
England country goods, in the rough arms of the Green Mountains.
He had just finished college and turned twenty-two that summer.
He had won a fellowship to spend a month in a poetry workshop
with nine other writers from all over the country. It was an annual
contest. Hundreds of applicants submitted ten poems each, and the
ten winners were hand picked by the patriarch of the nation's poets,
Walter Craft, who seemed to Lance a living extension of the previous century—although Craft was only twelve when that century
had ended. They were given free tuition, room, and board. Jeremiah
McCloy wasn't picked for the seminar and decided to go back home
and paint his parents' house instead. The ten of them, the chosen
young poets, arrived in the middle of June and kept to themselves
for a month—an elite workshop among the paying students who had
other writing teachers.

The writing school's campus was a mile up the road from the
village where Craft had a summer house. The students called Craft's
village the incest capital of New England. The miniature campus
had three long dormitories, a little white chapel, and several smaller
buildings with seminar rooms and faculty offices. When it wasn't
raining, classes were held outside on the lawn. This writing school
was part of a college located in the valley down below; in winter it
accommodated students who came up to ski, but in the summer the
writers took over. On one edge of the campus was a narrow road that
drilled its way between two mountains; on the other, a forest and a
small trout stream that fed into a sleepy frog pond. A large part of
the lawn was strewn with oversize Adirondack chairs. Painted in
red and yellow, the chairs looked from afar like strokes of paint on
a grassy canvas.

The members of Craft's workshop would gather at ten in the morning for two hours and then eat lunch together; at three they would reconvene for another class in which they submitted new poems for a round-robin critique. Walter Craft presided over their discussions, favoring no one, giving advice only on form, never on subject matter. They all judged each other. They were, all ten of them, very good. And Tammy LaGrange was the most gifted one. Lance had understood this immediately, after hearing her read a poem about lessons in lovemaking given by a farmer's daughter from the Shenandoah Valley to a scion of southern aristocrats after they had met at the University of Virginia. Lance sought Tammy's company and friendship, and he soon knew enough about her past to read her poems as more than lyrical fictions.

Tammy was the first in her family to go to college. She had grown up on a dairy farm with four siblings and lots of animals. Her father had come back from Vietnam with two combat pals who were as lost and shaken as he was. The pals stayed on their farm for three months, drinking beer and malt alcohol, and left only after a few neighbors came over one evening with shotguns and asked to speak to Tammy's father. Soon after that, Tammy's mother started drinking. A meek and kindly man, Tammy's father was the one who protected Tammy, her sisters, and her little brother from their mother's drunkenness. The father's face would sometimes be bruised purple, his eye sockets crimson and swollen. He never hit his wife back. Fishing and hunting were his refuge.

Lance had never met anyone like Tammy while he was growing up in the Midwest or later while he was at Dartmouth. She represented a world he had known only from books and movies. Fields and arbors were more than a place for Tammy. They were her way of being. And she was a poet. In her poems there was green sunlight that felt warm on his skin, there were bales of hay that gave out a dizzying scent, there were goats whose names were Josephine and Henrietta and who knew all about their owners' drinking and fighting and about country baking with lots of butter and sour cream. In her poems Lance could stroll and breathe and lose himself, and they made him forget that they were not real, not life or so-called life. Tammy LaGrange knew—instinctively—how to hide the seams of being.

By the end of the first week Lance and Tammy had become a couple in their peers' eyes. And in their own? After breakfast, before their morning class, they went for hikes up a trail that led to an oval meadow overgrown with cornflowers. In the meadow they would talk about poetry and their families. She described the forlorn songs her mother sometimes sang while strumming the guitar— when she was about to go on a binge. He reminisced about growing up in Cleveland—the lake, his father's pharmacy, the all-state spelling bee he had won in sixth grade. Together they made fun of the other poets in their workshop and of Walter Craft's tired aphorisms. Tammy had left the state of Virginia only once before college, and Lance told her about his semester at Oxford and about seeing Paris and Rome and Barcelona. They sat next to each other in the cafeteria, and after lunch they pulled together a couple of the Adirondack chairs and composed side by side. On the lawn Lance gave Tammy a lesson in fly-fishing—the art he had learned while at Dartmouth and was proud of—and they went fishing for rainbows upstream from the campus. They showed each other all their new poems first, before making copies for the rest of the group. Lance moralized in his, reflecting on history and politics, usually in first person, and even back then his poems were perfectly crafted, like a Swiss pocket watch: one opened the golden lid and stared at the filigreed face, having forgotten that the piece actually told time. "Gorgeous," Tammy would usually say after reading his poem. And about her poems he would often say, "Remarkable." He especially admired Tammy's love poems: the nakedness, the fairy-tale suspense, the unhappy endings.

Lance remembered a misty night he and Tammy went for a long walk after seeing a production of *Midsummer Night's Dream* by the playwriting students. They had been sitting in a stuffy chapel for three hours, and both wanted to catch some air. They walked downhill on a narrow road that sparkled like tin under the moon, and Lance touched her hand, then took it. Tammy turned and gave him a bemused smile. The road took a bend, and a clay path branched off to the right, into grass and darkness.

"You want to go this way?" he asked Tammy.

"Okay," she whispered.

The moon was behind a mountain peak, and in darkness they moved like two sleepwalkers toward the outlines of haystacks. The grass felt bristly and wet on Lance's ankles. He stopped and brought his left hand around Tammy's waist. He pulled her closer, and their bodies came together.

"What will your girlfriend say?" Tammy whispered.

"I can't help it, Tammy."

They kissed with a fervor that Lance thought he still remembered on his lips so many years later. They must have kissed for an hour standing under a dim summer night sky. He now had his hands under her skirt, the edges of his palms feeling the rims and slopes of her body. A few feet away a haystack loomed in darkness.

After they got up, as they were brushing blades of grass and strings of hay off their clothes, Tammy called his name.

"Drew?"

"Yeah?"

"This isn't right," she said loudly.

"What?"

"We can't do this."

"I know, I know. I'll tell Jill, I promise."

"When?"

"I'll talk to her when she comes to visit in two weeks."

"Why not sooner?"

"I don't know if I can break it to her on the telephone," he answered sullenly.

After that night and the haystack Lance thought that Tammy would pull back, but she didn't. They still went on their morning hikes to their meadow, and they still composed side by side on the green, trusting each other with drafts of their newest poems. She never brought up the subject of Lance's girlfriend for the next two weeks, and despite the ardent tension, Lance was content with the unsaid and with Tammy's company.

Then Jill came up to see Lance at the end of the program in the middle of July. There was an old tradition at the writing school—a celebration at which the participants would read from their new work: poets to other poets, fiction writers to other fiction writers. Jill had wanted to be at the readings, and they had planned a motoring trip to Montreal and Quebec City. She and Lance had been going steady since their junior year at Dartmouth. At first, Lance hadn't been sure what to make of the zeal with which she had pursued him. She had been attending readings of the student poetry society that he ran, memorizing his poems, befriending his roommates. Jill was slim, gray-eyed, a blue-blood Bostonian. Her father, grandfather, and elder brother were all maritime lawyers. Lance never felt much at ease in their company when he and Jill would drive down to Boston from New Hampshire for a day visit. By graduation time their friends sensed the impending engagement; in the fall Lance was starting an MFA at Brown, and Jill had chosen Harvard Law School over Yale to stay nearer to him. . . .

She arrived after lunch when he was taking a nap. She walked into his garret room wearing khakis, a white blouse, and a thin leather hair band, bringing with her an air of certainty and resolve.

"Show me your new poems," she commanded tenderly, after giving him a report on apartment hunting.

Lance pointed to a batch lying on the small desk by the window. Jill quickly read the top two. "You never used to write about trees and butterflies," she said, sitting down on his squeaky bed.

"Did you have lunch?" Lance asked.

"I stopped at a little sandwich shop after I got off the interstate."

"Do you want me to show you around?"

"Yes, later this afternoon," she said, kissing him on the cheek. "I'll go for a run now. And then I'll take a shower." Standing behind a half-open closet door, Jill changed into running clothes. Before leaving, she kissed him on the nape. "Back in half an hour or so. Love you."

She hadn't been gone five minutes when Tammy knocked on his door.

"I brought a new poem. Do you mind looking at it?"

"Of course not," Lance said, trying to sound chipper. He had told Tammy that Jill was coming in the afternoon. He had been preparing Jill, Lance said, by describing to her Tammy's poetry and their friendship. But, he said, he hadn't had the heart to tell Jill about the haystack.

Barefoot, Tammy was wearing a sleeveless shirt and a long limp skirt through which her legs showed white. "Here," she said, handing him two hand-written pages of five-line stanzas. "It's a bit longish. And I tried to rhyme."

Lance, still sitting on his bed, laid the pages on his knees. Tammy stood by the window swaying and humming something. He finished reading the poem. "It's excellent, Tammy, excellent," he said. "And the half-rhymes are very fine."

"You like?" Tammy crossed the room and sat on the bed next to him curling her feet under her.

"I like it. A lot."

"What're you reading tomorrow?" she asked.

"Jill's here, Tammy," Lance said without looking up.

"Where is she?"

"Out for a run."

"Did you tell her?"

"Not yet."

"You're going to?"

"Yes, later today. I think you'd better go now, Tammy."

"Okay."

And then, like in films where directors stab their characters in the back with daggers of chance, the door opened, and Jill came in.

"Jill," Lance got up, "this is my friend Tammy LaGrange. The poet I've told you about." He moved to the middle of the room, between the door and the bed.

"Delighted," Jill said icily. "And how are you going to introduce me, Andrew? As your friend Jill Lorimer, the runner you've told her about? This is just great: three friends gathered for tea and some poetry." Red blots spread over Jill's face and neck, which were already sweaty and pink from her run.

"Must you?" Lance intoned, looking neither at her nor at Tammy.

"Of course I must. You think I don't know what's going on here? You think I'm *that* thick?"

"Actually you don't know," Tammy said, but Jill interrupted her.

"Let me finish," she said, clenching her fists. "You think men go for you because you can write a few poems about cute prancing lambies, drunk rednecks, and losing your virginity at fourteen in a dark stable? You really think men go for you because they like your poems? That's not why. They like—"

"Jill!" Lance yelled. "That's enough!"

Lips shaking, Tammy turned to the door. She put her hand on the door knob and turned, facing Jill. "I had feelings for Drew, you're right about that. But Drew, he just wanted to be friends. And he was a good friend to me. Nothing more. He's a good man, your Drew. Hang on to him."

Tammy ran out of the room.

Lance spent the rest of the day trying to pacify Jill. They talked in his room for a long time. Then he took her to dinner in the neighboring town.

"What she said earlier, is it true?" Jill asked in the car on the way back.

"Yes, darling, of course it's true. Tammy's a friend. And a talented poet. We read and critique each other's poems."

"Read and critique," Jill repeated. "She was sitting on your bed when I returned from my run."

"Come on, Jill. You're being jealous."

"I don't trust her."

Tammy wasn't at the gala reading the next day, and Lance learned from a woman in their workshop that she had packed her things and left in the morning. He never heard from her after that summer. Nor did he try to get in touch with her. It all had happened a long time ago, and he almost felt as if it had happened to somebody else, somebody whom he had once known but had later forgotten. Trying to unremember Tammy and that summer in the Green Mountains—as well as Jill's jealousy and his own acquiescence—Lance finally fell into a haystack of dreamless sleep.

HE SLEPT UNTIL AFTER TEN and barely had enough time to grab a muffin and tea on the way to the campus. McCloy's poetry seminar was held in a dark room with an oval table. There were more women than men in the class of twelve. Lance talked for about twenty minutes, first about the importance of craft, then about the way personal experience "sears" poems with a "brand of authenticity." It all bordered on the platitudinal, and Lance knew it, but he was having such a hard time concentrating that he was grateful that at least a section of his mind had remained free of Tammy and was now feeding his vocal cords with cadences of advice to young poets.

Then Lance asked each student to read a poem. He nodded as they read, but didn't keep up with the beat of the students' poems. His nodding reproduced the rhythm of his own memory. Tam-my. Stalemate. Tam-my. Tame me. Tam-my. At the end of the seminar, he forgot to perform his ritual of asking the students to give him their work for the quarterly. This time, McCloy had to remind him, and Lance waited with a guilty smile while one of the students collected the submissions. Then he rose up, put them into a folder bound in morocco leather, and deposited the folder into his briefcase.

"What's wrong, Andy?" McCloy asked after the last student walked out of the room. "Not feeling well?"

"Just a bad night of insomnia. You ever get it?"

"Not really. Do you still want to have lunch at my house?"

"Of course, Jerry. Absolutely. I want to see Molly. I'll rest in the afternoon."

"What time's your plane tomorrow?"

"At 3:40, from Dulles. I plan to go fishing in the morning, on the way back."

"I'd join you, but I made plans to go bird-watching with a friend who teaches at St. Helen's. Derek Gill. Remember him?"

"Sure. Tall guy, red hair, freckles. Merrill chose his first book for the Younger Poets Prize. Hasn't done much since."

They drove to McCloy's house, where a three-course lunch was served in a dining room with framed herbaria and landscape water-colors on periwinkle walls. After lunch Lance had to endure an hour of Molly's stories about her talented students. McCloy's wife was a principal at the local high school, and Lance felt that his friend was slightly embarrassed of his wife's profession. When the cuckoo clock announced three, Lance began to twitch his fingers. McCloy, who sensed that something was going on, offered to take him back.

"You're okay, Andy?" he asked again as he pulled up to the lodge.

"I don't know, Jerry. I'm sorry I botched up your seminar."

"Don't worry about it."

"I'll e-mail you next week. And about the students' poems, too."

"Stop by tonight after supper if you feel like it. Have a good trip, Andy."

Lance was in his room at 3:30. He called the front desk asking about messages.

"No messages, sir," said a high-pitched female voice.

"Are you sure?"

"Pretty sure. Been here all day."

Lance sat in the armchair, then got up and started pacing between door to window. Then he opened his briefcase, removed the morocco leather folder, and took out the top page. His eyes slid across the surface, jumping from one stanza to the next. The poem was about horses, and Lance thought it annoying and predictable. He tried a poem from the middle of the batch, but found it tedious, the rhymes awkward like a pimply teenager, the metaphors jarring. He paced some more, then lay down on his bed in clothes and loafers and closed his eyes. The phone rang at four.

"Tammy? Hi! Where are you?"

"I'm at home."

"I was worried I'd missed your call."

"You haven't."

"Do you still want to meet?"

"Sure."

"What's a good restaurant in town?"

"Well, Giorgio's is supposed to be very good. Expensive though."

"How expensive can things be around here?"

"Still a snob, Drew."

"What time?"

"My husband is taking the kids to a basketball game at Staunton. Why don't we meet in the restaurant at 7:30?"

Lance looked up Giorgio's in the phone book and called for a reservation. He undressed. He wanted to shower but decided to call home first.

"You sound tired," Jill said in her unwavering voice. "How did the reading go? How's Jerry?"

"Fine, fine. I'm going out for supper, and tomorrow I'm getting up at the crack of dawn to go fishing. Just wanted to say hello."

"Andrew, you sound funny."

"I didn't sleep well last night. And I left my sleeping pills at home. In the bathroom."

"Maybe you should take a break from these campus trips."

"Perhaps you're right."

"We are quite solvent, you know. And your magazine gets more submissions than you can read in your lifetime."

"I'll think about it, darling. I promise. See you tomorrow?"

"We're all coming to the airport to get you. Catch some fish. Bye."

Lance woke up from a nap feeling less anxious. He went out for a stroll, got a cup of watery coffee at an ice cream parlor, and returned to his room. He showered and shaved a second time, put on cologne, and dressed slowly and pensively—a mercury gray shirt, cords, a black cashmere V-neck. The restaurant was in the downtown area, and after getting directions at the reception desk, he decided to walk. It took about twenty minutes. The restaurant turned out to be in a pedestrian area of several blocks lined with arched streetlamps and cast-iron bollards. Well-dressed couples were strolling there, the men in suits and hats. Retro, Lance thought as he walked past an art gallery to the restaurant.

At Giorgio's, a chunky maître d' showed Lance to a table by the window, which had a good view of the walking area. A table light made of blue glass cast a thin shadow across his plate. Lance leaned his head against the window and peered into the street. Babbly skirts and pants. Male and female silhouettes flitting by. Hazy yellow lights. Rendezvous.

"Drew," Tammy's raspy voice startled Lance.

She wore a long black skirt with red arabesques, a velvet top, and a necklace of gray freshwater pearls. Her hair was French-braided this time.

"You look very nice," Lance said. He summoned the waiter and ordered a bottle of Pinot Noir.

"We don't usually come to this area," Tammy said after she took a sip of wine from a tall glass that she held with both hands. "Pricey."

Lance nodded.

"Caleb, my husband, works for the utilities company."

"I see. Does he know you're here?"

"No, does Jill?"

"No, I mean she knows I'm out to supper. Wait, how do you know Jill's my wife?"

"It's in the bio blurb in your book. Unless it's a different Jill."

"No, same Jill." Bridging an awkward pause, he asked, "How old are your kids?"

"Nat's fourteen, and Abigail will be twelve next spring."

"Mine are thirteen and eleven. Also a boy and a girl."

"Does Jill work?"

"Yes, she's an attorney. Devilishly active. Are you working?"

"Course I am, I have to. Caleb drinks. Less now than before. He used to stay home and drink for several days straight. But he's got golden hands, he can fix anything. That's why they haven't fired him."

"How's your mother?" Lance asked, remembering Tammy's family stories.

"She died three years ago, of liver failure."

"I'm so sorry."

"That's okay. My dad is doing pretty well. He remarried and moved to Lynchburg."

"You haven't said anything about your work, Tammy."

"I'm a kindergarten teacher."

"I see."

Lance put a piece of bittersweet salmon in his mouth. The salmon appetizer had been baked on a cedar plank with coriander seeds.

"I know you're shocked and trying not to show it," Tammy said. "It's all right, Drew. A lot has changed in seventeen years."

"It's just that . . . well, why aren't—"

"Why aren't I where we thought I'd be? Publishing poetry and winning awards like you? Well, things just didn't turn out that way."

"When did you get married?" Lance asked.

"The fall after I finished college—and met you. Caleb's a distant cousin on my mother's side. We grew up together. He's a good man."

They talked some more about their families and marriages.

"Are you still writing?" Lance asked what he had wanted to ask her the whole time.

"Sure, from time to time."

"Are you sending things out?"

"No."

"Why not?"

"The same reason I can't deal with many other things. I tried teaching high school. The kids are okay, but the teachers. . . . I tried the local paper too."

"All it takes is putting a few poems in an envelope."

"I can't take ugly rejection slips. Not now. I'm almost forty and—"

"So why didn't you write to me at the quarterly?" Lance interrupted her.

"A couple of years ago," Tammy continued, ignoring his question, "I got a letter from a Josephine Levinson, who teaches women's studies at a college up in Maine. She'd found a poem of mine in an old issue of *Shenandoah* from 1981, when I was a junior in college. She said she wanted to know more about me and my work. I never wrote back. What's the point?"

"Tammy, you were good. Oh, damn it, you were the best in our seminar. You had your own voice, whatever the hell that means!" Lance threw his blazer on the back of his chair.

"Thanks, Drew, I know you really admired my poems. I never quite figured out why. I thought yours were so much better. Elegant, shapely."

"Who cares about all that? Your poems were alive. They sparkled."

"I just wrote them as they came to me."

"Listen, Tammy, I'll make a deal with you. You give me a bunch of poems to take home with me, and I'll run a selection in the next issue. You'll see, you'll have editors calling you."

"I don't know."

"I'll tell you what else I'll do. After your poems come out in the magazine, I'll send them with a note to my editor at Norton. Deal?"

"You're sweet. Let me think about it."

"Don't think about it. Just go home and bring me some poems. Let's meet for breakfast tomorrow morning, and you'll give me the poems."

"I don't know, Drew."

"What's a place to get breakfast around here?"

"Well, there's Moosley's, at Laurel and Washington."

"Great. Meet me there at 7:30. I'm going fly-fishing and then straight to the airport."

"Okay."

They said good-bye outside the restaurant. Lance went back to the hotel on foot, sipping the misty air, humming a Verdi aria.

A lettuce green, two-door Ford Granada was parked in front of his room when he arrived there. Tammy was sitting on the hood, smoking and playing with her hair.

"Tammy?" Lance said, voice trembling.

"Hi there."

"Do you want to come in?"

He unlocked the door and let Tammy in first. His hand was feeling around for the switch on the wall.

"Don't turn on the light." He felt her hand on his neck and cheek. "Oh, Drew," she exhaled, pressing her body to his.

Afterward they silently lay in darkness, she smoking, he sipping water from a plastic bottle he kept at his side. Then the phone rang, and he didn't answer.

"That's probably Jill," said Lance.

"I hope you don't tell her now."

"I don't know."

"You would've been better off with a Jewish girl," Tammy half-whispered, sliding her fingers across his forehead and down his face to his chest. "See you tomorrow, Drew."

LANCE WOKE UP at 6:30 feeling fresh and renewed, but also dimly anxious. He packed his things, put on khakis, a red turtleneck, a fishing vest, and hiking boots. The day looked perfect for fishing: sun coming up through wispy clouds, not a tremor in the leaves, the air dry and scented with autumnal withering.

He asked for directions to Moosley's, and the night receptionist gave him a strange look while explaining how to get there. For about ten minutes Lance zigzagged through empty streets looking for the intersection of Laurel and Washington. Moosley's turned out to be a rusty diner next door to a pool hall. In contrast to the groomed lawns and homes around the campus, the area struck Lance as depressed, the homes shabby, the building facades squalid and unpainted for too long. He walked into the diner and looked across the room. It was 7:35. An elderly couple was eating pancakes at a corner table, and three men, two of them wearing overalls, occupied the left side of the counter.

Lance sat at the counter on a cracked red vinyl seat and asked for some tea with lemon.

"I'm waiting for somebody," he told the middle-aged waitress in a dirty apron.

"Take your time. Going fishing?"

"Yes, after breakfast."

One of the fellows in overalls gave Lance a grim look from under his slabs of eyebrows.

After waiting for about twenty minutes, Lance ordered eggs and toast.

"Any bacon or ham?" asked the waitress.

"No thanks, just the check, please."

Lance quickly ate his breakfast, washed it down with the tasteless tea, and put a five-dollar bill on the counter. He threw another long look across the room, as if hoping Tammy might be reading the paper at one of the tables.

"Good luck fishing," the waitress said so loudly that the other customers turned his way. Lance nodded silently and walked out.

He got into the rental car and slammed the door. Leaving behind the college town, he drove north on an empty county road for about half an hour. He checked the directions to the state park that he had printed off the Internet. After Townsend Farms there was supposed to be a sign and a turn to a gravel road. "There it is, Clear Brook State Park," Lance muttered and hit the brakes. The road into which he turned went up into the wooded hills. After driving for about five miles—gravel and milky dust coming up from under his wheels—he stopped at a little store, really no more than a log cabin set back about fifteen yards off the road. He walked into the store expecting a toothless old man with a bristly swinish face. Instead, he saw a girl of about thirteen or fourteen, dark-haired, with cat eyes. Sitting behind the counter on a high stool, she held a decrepit paperback in her hands.

"Miss, I was wondering if I could buy a fishing permit for one day?" Lance asked the girl.

"The shortest we have is one week," the girl replied showing coral white teeth. "Would you like one?"

"Yes, please. I'm only going to fish for a few hours though."

"It's ten dollars. Plus another five for a trout stamp."

The girl tore off a little form for him to fill out and asked for his driver's license. She put the bottom copy of the permit into an old cash register with large round keys.

"What's a good place to fly-fish?" Lance asked.

"Go up the road for half a mile. You'll see a trail going off to your left. Park the car and go up the trail until you hit the stream. There are flat rocks you can cast off of. My dad likes that spot. He's the warden here."

"Do you know what they're hitting on?"

"Right now they're mighty hungry. Whatever you have, not too small, not too big. I hear ants work pretty good."

"Thanks." Not knowing why, Lance extended his hand to the girl for a handshake.

He followed the directions and found the trail the girl had described. He opened the trunk of his car and took the rod out of its case. After feeding the line through the rings, he tied on a tippet, then a fly, a black imitation ant. The trail turned out to be longer than he had expected. Finally, he heard the gurgling of the stream, then saw clear spaces beyond the pine trunks. "There it is," he said to himself out loud.

He climbed onto a mossy rock whose lip hung over the stream. He stood there studying the water until he heard a splash to the left of him. Moving quietly and slowly, he walked over to the next rock downstream, then the next one, and continued this way until he found a perfect spot: a flat rock to stand on and enough space around him to cast. To the left near the opposite bank of the stream there was a pool of clear brownish water to which the current brought red leaves and yellow pine needles. Lance cast upstream and waited for the current to carry his fly to the pool. He cast several times, then put on a new fly made of elk bristle. Hot from hiking and casting, he took a sip of water from a bottle stored in one of his vest pockets. A bird carried its thin trill across the stream into the thickets on the opposite bank. Lance heard another splash.

He cast upstream and waited, watching his fly twitch as the current took possession of it. When the fly reached the middle of the pool, Lance saw a splash, and his fly went under. "There you are, my sweet. There you are," he whispered, collecting the slack into the reel. He felt a series of pulls. Pangs. "You're beautiful, my sweet. My rainbow. And you love this fly. And I love you." He let her fight and kick and tire herself. Then he reeled her in and netted her, landing his first trout of the day. In his hands the trout sparkled, wet and tremulous, like those poems Lance would never write.

Sonetchka

SONETCHKA'S E-MAIL came on April 12, the old Soviet Cosmonautics Day. It displayed an economy of words: "I've moved to Conn., a systems admin. job. The rest when I see you. SM."

Simon called Sonetchka and drove down from Providence to see her three days later, on a sunny Saturday morning. She was living in a condo in West Hartford, an affluent and conspicuously Jewish area. After getting off the highway, he passed two synagogues on the way to her place. Groups of Orthodox Jews were walking to shul. Women and young girls wore ankle-length skirts. Men in fedoras or derbies carried embroidered pillows under their arms. Driving through Sonetchka's new neighborhood, Simon thought of a life of stability and tradition.

He parked his beat-up Toyota in front of Sonetchka's condo compound and walked up to the front door. Her gendered Slavic name, "Mironova," looked foreign amid the wreath of markedly Jewish names such as "Goldstein" and "Rubin." He pressed the buzzer, and almost immediately he heard her voice, small and a bit husky, sounding as though it came from across the Atlantic Ocean.

"Syoma, *eto ty?*" (She called Simon by a diminutive of "Semyon," his Russian name.)

"Yes, Sonetchka, it's me."

"Come on up."

He ran up a carpeted staircase to the third floor. Sonetchka was standing in the doorway, resting her head and left shoulder against the half-opened wooden door that she was holding with her right hand. She was smiling, a fretful smile. Her wheaten hair was long and straight, and both her eye shadow and lipstick were of the same opaque, red brick color. Wearing a ribbed beige turtleneck, a pair of black stretchy pants, and suede penny loafers, she looked un-Russian, like a self-confident yuppie with a dash of prep. And yet there was something ethereal about Sonetchka, as though the forces of gravity didn't have a firm grip on her slender frame.

Simon and Sonetchka kissed and hugged each other. A wave of her perfumed hair washed against his cheek. Her fingers ran down his spine like a pianist's over a keyboard.

"Well, well, Sonetchka. How long has it been?"

"Almost nine years. Come in. I made good coffee."

She led him through the foyer into a bright living room, furnished with light beech furniture that made the space look bigger and more airy. A white leather couch and a matching armchair stood near the window. He saw a cobalt blue coffee set on a low table, and a large, overflowing ashtray in the shape of a flatfish. Sonetchka went to the kitchen and brought in a carafe of coffee. They sat down on the sofa.

"I want to hear all about you."

"You will," Sonetchka said. "But first, I wanted to tell you that I read your essay in *Harper's*. I was in the local bookstore browsing in the magazine section and saw your name on the cover."

"The one about Felix Kron?"

"Yes, the Jewish writer from Prague. I hadn't heard of him."

"He's my big thing," Simon said and nodded with contentment.

"You've come a long way, Simon B. Finn," Sonetchka said without irony in her voice. "Writing in English. Ivy League universities. When you're a famous professor, I'm going to tell everyone that I knew you at tender eighteen."

"We'll see. With this job market, let's hope I become a professor at all."

"You will, you've always known what you wanted from life. People like you always get what they deserve." The last sentence sounded bitter, but Simon knew Sonetchka didn't mean it like that.

She put a piece of crumbly blueberry cake on his plate.

"I baked it last night. I've only started to cook again since I moved up here from New York. It's a strange feeling to be cooking just for yourself."

"I know," Simon said. "I've been doing it since I started graduate school. Now tell me about coming to America. What happened to you guys?"

"Where do I start?" She lit a thin brown cigarette. "You probably heard from good old Misha Martov and various others how Igor and I got married."

"I heard some things and had to reconstruct the rest."

"I don't expect you to understand. You've never been a sucker for unlucky people."

"I actually do understand it perfectly well. Igor was in the military. You rescued him. It's classic."

"And stupid. You'd emigrated. I was in some sort of daze when I went to see him while he was away in the army in Belarus and then when he was home on furlough for the wedding. Igor took care of all the arrangements. His parents were dead set against it, telling him that I would be a rock tied to his neck. That I would ruin his life. That I was merely trying to snag a nice Jewish boy."

The phone rang. Sonetchka let it ring until the answering machine picked up, but the caller didn't leave a message. Simon took off his shoes and stretched his legs on the coffee table.

"Let me get you a pillow," Sonetchka suggested. "This is going to take a while."

She came back from the bedroom with a velvet pillow that she placed under the nape of his head, after brushing her hand through his hair.

"After Igor was demobilized in the summer of 1989, we rented a room so as not to stay with his parents. For a few months things weren't too bad, but then Igor's parents finally decided to emigrate, and Igor said we were going too. It was easier for him—he wasn't leaving family behind in Moscow. We left in the fall, on a drizzly October morning. I couldn't stop crying, and Igor was angry with both me and his parents."

"I remember that day very well," Simon said quietly. "I mean, I remember the day *my* family left Moscow. It was awful, the airport, border control, all of you guys waving from the other side. My parents' friends, too. My mom wept the whole time."

"At least you got to leave with your parents. I . . . "

"I know," Simon said. "I mean, I don't know," he added guiltily.

"It was pretty horrible," Sonetchka continued with her story. "We arrived in New York in November and went to live in Queens. Igor's father had an older sister in Forest Hills. We lived in a two-bedroom apartment together with Igor's parents. I got a data-entry job and took evening computer classes for a year. Then I started working at a bank, and things were going pretty well for me professionally. For two years I pretty much supported them. I was making a good salary, really, and at first I didn't so much mind being the breadwinner. Igor's parents could speak no English. His mother did some clothes alterations and—"

"—Oh, sure," Simon interrupted, "I remember she used to do that back in Moscow. Whenever Misha and I would come over, she would always be knitting a sweater for a client or fixing a cuff or a lining. That's the main thing I remember about her. That and her fishy eyes."

Sonetchka looked at him with surprise.

"Igor's father couldn't find work as an engineer, so he began to clean offices and restaurant bathrooms with a crew of other Russians. He started drinking heavily, and when he was drunk, he would call me "shiksa" and "Russian slut." His mom just looked away, racing her sewing machine. If Igor happened to be home at the time, he would stick up for me and threaten to break his dad's neck if he didn't shut up. But later, when we were alone, he told me that I provoked his father and that he was losing his mind between the hammer and the anvil. And at other times when Igor's father got wasted, he—the father—would kiss my hands, get down on his knees, and ask me to forgive him. Can you believe it?"

"Yes. No," Simon replied, trying not to blush as he felt responsibility for this *shikker*, as his paternal grandmother would call a Jewish drunkard—responsibility and also shame.

"It was awful, just awful!" Sonetchka said after pouring herself more coffee from the carafe. "I begged Igor to get our own apartment, and we eventually moved. Igor was barely on speaking terms with his father at that point. The worst of it was that Igor refused to finish college—and he would have had only two more years to go if he had transferred his Moscow credits. I implored him. He was terrified of failure, of not being able to compete with American students. You know how strong-willed he used to be when you were still friends."

"All of us used to think he had iron will and nerves of steel," Simon said, piling one Russian cliché on top of the other.

"Well, it's as if he left his willpower in Moscow."

"Sonetchka, this happens to many immigrants. It's quite common."

"But it didn't have to happen to us."

She got up from the sofa and threw a white wool shawl over her shoulders.

"So we lived this way for three more years. I was working and making quite a bit of money. Igor began to drive a cab, mostly at night, and during the day he slept, read—"

"—What did he read?" Simon asked, interrupting Sonetchka again.

"Funny you should ask. Mainly the classics, Tolstoy, Turgenev, Goncharov. And lots of Bunin. You were crazy about Bunin when we met."

"Yeah, *Dark Avenues* was one of my favorite books," Simon answered dreamily. "But I can't read it now. The same with Hesse."

"My tastes have also changed here. Or is it the age? In any case, when he wasn't working, Igor read a lot and watched Russian films on video. And he also hung out with a couple of Russian buddies who, like himself, were having a hard time adjusting to their new lives. We didn't see much of each other during the week. I would be out of the apartment by 7:30, and Igor's night shift usually began at 5:00 in the afternoon. We did try to do things together on weekends. I remember, one time, we went up to Vermont to ski."

"When did you learn to ski?" Simon asked.

"I didn't. I mean, I didn't that time. On the way up there we got into a huge fight in the car over something trivial, and Igor ended up skiing alone while I sat in our motel room, smoked, and watched TV for two days."

Sonetchka lit another cigarette, then continued.

"There isn't much else to tell, I'm afraid. We grew farther and farther apart, going for months without making love. He was too proud to ask for it, and I was too withdrawn to seduce him, even though sex could sometimes mend things between us. I tried to get pregnant, but nothing came of it. I guess our marriage just wasn't meant to be from the very beginning. Doomed. I wanted us to move out of New York to a suburb, but he wouldn't hear of it. By the fall of last year our conversations had been reduced to a mere formality. Then I had an affair with a French guy at work—a very nice guy, really, and it gave me strength. Then I knew I had to leave Igor."

"How did he take it?" Simon asked.

"At first he was livid. Then he started saying all these self-deprecating things, blaming everything on himself. He wanted to work things out, he said. It was too late, I told him. I already had a lawyer filing papers for divorce. And I got a great job offer from the First Bank of Hartford. I'm director of systems administration."

"That sounds prosperous. Did he try to get you to pay alimony?"

"No, he's not like that. Igor has many problems, but he does have a noble soul."

"I see," Simon said bemusedly because it had been a long time since he had last heard anyone use this expression. "A noble soul, hmm . . . yes, that and a heart of gold."

"Don't be sarcastic, please, Syoma."

Sonetchka walked to the French doors and pressed her forehead to the glass. The sun was no longer falling into the room. Outside, a brook looped its way through the gnarled feet of the old elm trees. On the manicured lawn, young crocuses were shooting up white and lilac.

"I like it here," Sonetchka said, letting out a long wisp of smoke. "It's very peaceful. I never thought I'd so much enjoy being alone. Anyhow, we should probably go get a bite to eat. I know a great lunch place only a few minutes from here."

They drove in Sonetchka's brand-new Saab to a little restaurant overlooking a lake and a pine grove. Families with small kids sat eating their lunches, unhurriedly and contentedly, and to the parents Sonetchka and Simon probably looked like a young couple testing the waters of married life. After lunch the two of them made a full circle around the lake, and Simon told Sonetchka about his nine years in America and about the biography of Felix Kron he was hoping to write. He also told her a bit about his own love life, about his engagement to Nora Frick and their breakup, about the six months he had spent in Prague in 1992. Of course, Simon thought, these were only stories to Sonetchka, stories as fictional and as distant from her as the ones she might read in novels or see in movies, whereas her life with Igor was as real to Simon as his own life. Sonetchka *was* a part of his life.

They were standing near an empty playground with three sets of swings, a sandbox, and a sea-saw. A menagerie of clouds was drifting west over their heads—kangaroos, bears, elephants, and even a fat boa constrictor. The red bobber of a boy's fishing line was going up and down on the lake's steel surface. In the pine grove a woodpecker was keeping time with the bobber's convulsions.

"Listen, Sonetchka," Simon said, feeling a surge of something so acute and yet so hidden in the depths of memory. "This may not be a good time to say it, but I may never again get myself to do it. I'm sorry I was such an arrogant bastard back in Russia. I'm sorry I treated you so cruelly. I didn't know any better at the time. I was just a spoiled Moscow tomcat who was playing at chivalry. Please forgive me if you can."

"Syoma, my dear baby boy, I forgave you a long time ago. I just wish it was you I got to leave Russia with."

They looked at each other and smiled when they saw the tears in each other's eyes. They hugged and stood there on the lake shore, gently stroking each other's backs and shoulders. Over the heads of Simon and Sonetchka, a flock of Canadian geese carried north their shrieks of longing.

They drove back to Sonetchka's place, and Simon helped her make a simple dinner: twice-baked chicken (his mother's recipe), roasted potatoes and onions, a mesclun salad with grape tomatoes and crumbled blue cheese. While the food was cooking, they sat on the sofa, arms over each other's shoulders, and drank a bottle of Chianti that had a faint strawberry nose. A plaid wool blanket covered their feet. The phone rang several times, but Sonetchka ignored it. After supper they went back to the sofa, sat next to each other, drank jasmine tea, and ate thin sugar biscuits with apricot preserves. They reminisced about Russia, about their childhood, about the summers they used to spend with their parents in Pärnu, on the west coast of Estonia. And they remembered their group of Pärnu friends who had met at the beach when they were five or six. . . . Then it was time for Simon to drive back to Providence, and he made Sonetchka promise she would call him if she needed anything.

"Come to see me in Prov," Simon said. "I won't be there for much longer. I'm waiting to hear from the places I interviewed with. Who knows where I'll end up going? Laramie, Wyoming? Flagstaff, Arizona? End of the world?"

"There is no end of the world here in America," Sonetchka said.

When he was walking out the door, he turned around and asked her: "Sonetchka, do you remember our picnic on Misha Martov's eighteenth birthday?"

"Silly boy, of course I do," said Sonetchka with passion. "All of you: Misha, Igor, you, and fat Andrey had hard-ons when you were getting out of the water. God, I was seventeen, just finished high school. We were practically children."

Simon kissed her on the forehead.

"Remember, Sonetchka," he said, pressing his hands to her cheeks and looking into her pale green eyes. "Back in Russia, I once told you we'd always be each other's special friends. Summertime romance sometimes bonds people for life."

"Bye, Syoma. Drive carefully. Bye."

He drove back to Providence on an empty highway, printing pictures from the negatives of his memory, recalling details of that last blissful Estonian summer. Simon then remembered that during his first months in America, when nostalgia would ripple across his heart, he used to think, not without jealousy, that Sonetchka had taken his place in their brotherhood of Moscow friends. But he was wrong, he now understood: it wasn't his place that Sonetchka had taken, it was Igor's, while Igor himself had faded away into oblivion, first vanishing from Simon's own life, then from Sonetchka's . . .

During the next two weeks Simon telephoned Sonetchka several times, only to talk to her answering machine, and then things got crazy with the job search. At the end of April, after he had accepted a tenure-track position at a college west of Boston, he drove up to look for an apartment. He was too early for an appointment with a rental broker in Brookline, so he went into a Russian bakery-café to kill half an hour. The proprietress, a turtle with the dovish eyes of an Odessan belle, asked him where he came from in the old country and what his *biznes* was up in Boston. After Simon had introduced myself with the affected cordiality that he sometimes poured on fellow émigrés—in the sense that it's fine to see other Russians in a strange land—the turtle-dove said she used to know his mother's half-sister during her days in the Bolshoy Ballet troupe. She served Simon a glazed poppy-seed roll on the house and wouldn't stop talking about his aunt's gorgeous legs. Simon ended up giving her his mother's number just to be rid of her and settled with a Russian daily paper near a rain-speckled window. He was almost finished with his coffee when his eyes wandered across a short article about a Russian cab driver who had murdered his ex-wife outside her apartment building in West Hartford.

The Afterlove

A MAN IN HIS LATE FORTIES stood out among the other guests at the long table. The festivities had reached a plateau: the guests had consumed much food and liquor, and yet half-empty plates and bottles still crowded the table. Only a few people continued eating and drinking. Fingers plucked slices of Hungarian salami, picked up glossy pieces of cured sturgeon, played with sprigs of coriander. Hands touched vodka and wine glasses, then brought them to lips with great effort, as though the glasses were filled with lead. Everyone felt tired after an evening of indulgent feasting. Socialites had already wrung the last drops from their conversations. A couple of flirtations, started with the help of the hostess and ignited by the spirits, now lingered at opposite ends of the table.

Pavel Lidin sat at the table under watercolors of mauve and blue. Actually, most of the guests knew him by the diminutive "Pavlik." In the hospitable home of Professor Fyodor Shtock, a well-known Moscow anthropologist, Pavel Lidin was a living legend. Some considered him brilliant, whereas others could only think of him as a court jester. All of them in Shtock's circle were born in the decade before World War II. No ethnic or national distinctions were made in their midst, and the Preobrazhenskys, the Fleishmans, the Leselidzes, the Sokols, the Ayvazians, the Krechetovs, and the Lidins would assemble at the Shtocks' five or six times a year, addicted to social rituals, as were many Muscovites.

Pavel Lidin always came with his wife, Alyona, a shadowy creature whom the others ignored—some gently, some sadistically. She never took part in conversations; drunk after one glass of wine, she would disappear into the kitchen, where more liquor would be waiting for her in the cupboard, usually a carafe of home-flavored ashberry vodka. Unlike his wife, Pavel never showed signs of inebriation. Each new drink gave him strength, and his mighty voice made the crystal on the candelabra resonate and jingle.

His mustache was the first thing to catch one's eye. Many men were jealous of his mustache. It made Pavel look like a Cossack: black with streaks of gray, perfectly groomed, three fingers thick, wiry. Like iron rims, it held together the barrel of his mouth. Next one noted Pavel's eyes: huge, deep set, oxish. There were also his large hands, levitating over the table, the wrists dark, the palms silvery. And his voice, his remarkable voice. Upon hearing it for the first time, one might have recognized several distinct elements in his singing. All-male chorus, an ancient Georgian tradition—thick and sonorous, love's birth and death, blood whirling with new wine. Ukrainian folk songs, "Come out, *kokhanaya* (my love), if only for a minute." Tart and teasing tunes. And finally, Chalyapin's basso, the brooding Czar Boris, a voice that makes one sober up and start one's life anew.

How did it happen that toward the end of that April evening in 1981 Pavel suddenly began to sing Siberian prisoners' songs? Had the hosts planned it? Had one of the witty guests talked Pavel into an unexpected performance? Rocking from side to side like a mad pendulum, Pavel sang about thieves and robbers, a topic no one in the room particularly cared for. After he started singing, his rickety wife came back from the kitchen and toppled onto her husband's shoulder. Soon tired of listening, the other guests began to whisper across the table, shaking off the songs' distressing words. Pavel continued to sing and sway. The only person captivated by the singing was the Shtocks' thirteen-year-old son, Kirill. Ending the song abruptly, Pavel lifted his head, and Kirill saw turbid tears in the corners of Pavel's eyes. The other guests got up from the table, shuf-fling their chairs, lighting cigarettes, and talking loudly and with relief. The dining room quickly grew empty.

Remaining at the table were Pavel, Alyona, who was now asleep in a chair, and Kirill. In the foyer Shtock was helping his guests with coats and paying the women final compliments in his profes-sorial voice. Then Shtock's wife cleared the dirty dishes and bot-tles, and brought in a tray with a Saxony teapot and cups as well as two desserts, an apple torte and a honey cheesecake. "Everyone left all at once. Well, I guess we'll have tea by ourselves," she sighed, pouring tea into china cups that were thin and translucent like Aly-ona's hands. Kirill was dying to ask Pavel a question, but he was a polite boy and didn't want to interrupt the adults. Finally, gathering enough courage, he blurted out: "Uncle Pavlik, how do you know all those jail songs?"

Pavel bared his perfect teeth, took a gulp of tea, swallowed a hunk of apple torte, and started to tell a long and circuitous story about working for two years at railroad construction in Siberia after he was at the university. "We rented a room and a half from an old guy who used to hide runaway prisoners. He gave them food and shelter. They had nothing to pay him back with but songs." Pavel talked a bit about his prewar Stalinist childhood, then about the war and the evacuation of his family to a remote village in the Ural Mountains, and then their return to Moscow in the summer of 1944. Whether it was because he was exhausted or extremely agitated, he mixed up places and years, jumping from '39 to '45, from '45 to '49. Then he completely forgot about the boy's question and—with replenished energy—began a new story.

"Listen, my boy," Pavel said, addressing Kirill. "Has your father ever told you about the summer of '45, about the experimental sum-mer camp?"

"No, never." Kirill's hazel eyes kept darting back and forth between Pavlik Lidin and his father. "Papa?"

"Sure, son, but there isn't much to tell," Shtock said twisting his lips. "I hated it there. It was a cold summer; my clothes were always damp."

"Papa! Is that why you wouldn't let me go to camp?"

"I wouldn't quite put it that way. But yes, son, I don't have very fond memories of summer camp. Uncle Pavlik, however, seems to have had a jolly time there. Pavlik, you tell it. I'll correct you if need be."

"Very good," Pavel smiled, ignoring Shtock's familiar sarcasm, and continued with his story. "During the spring of '45 they selected guys from all the high schools within the Boulevard Ring. Gym teachers tested us. Only the most physically fit were picked. We had to do chin-ups and climb ropes. Your father and I had just turned thirteen, but we both were already five eleven. And could do twenty chin-ups."

"Well, not twenty," Shtock corrected him. "Let's not go overboard with this. Ten, fifteen, perhaps."

"Okay, fifteen, whatever. Anyway, they selected about fifty guys, put us on buses, and on the first of June off we went. When we arrived, there was no campsite. Nothing. But the place was pristine—no one had been camping there during the war years. It was very quiet there, almost unreal. A lake shore. A pine forest. Bilberries, mushrooms. You must remember that we all were hungry after the war. So we built a summer camp, pitched our tents. We hadn't brought much with us: two sacks of potatoes and some grains. But nothing like canned pork or lard. The camp was experimental. Somebody from the Moscow school department decided that rather than having a bunch of young lads hang around the city, it would be better to ship us off to the country and have us procure our own daily bread. And we did: the lake was right there, so we fished an awful lot. The lake hadn't been fished during the war and was exploding with fish. We took our catch to local villages and bartered it for honey, milk, and vegetables. We ate really well that summer."

Pavel served himself a large piece of cheesecake, mouthed a third of the piece, and noisily drank some tea. Ready to go on, he was filling his chest with air when Shtock preempted him.

"My dear Pavlik, I've got a question for you. I remember everything from that summer—more or less. But, uh-hum, but the fish, the fish. . . . How did we manage to catch so much fish? Did we use nets?"

"Why nets? No," Pavel answered, quick to take offense. "We didn't need nets. Don't you remember? We had a better way. There was this guy, Seva Trofimov, who knew a lot about fishing. He was the one who taught us. This is what you do," and Pavlik glanced first at Kirill, who was listening with an open mouth, and then at Shtock. "You tie a mesh sack to your waist, take in as much air as your lungs can hold, dive in, and then look for caves under the shore. That's the secret: fish simply stay there waiting to be caught. If you insert your hand into one of the holes, you can feel their bodies trembling. They can't escape now since you've blocked their exit. You just start grabbing as many as you can and put them in your sack. Sometimes we'd get as many as five or six at a time. That's how we survived the whole summer."

"My friend," Shtock spoke in a giggly, nasal voice. "I've always, always liked your tales. Especially the ones where I myself appear as a character. A lucky fisherboy, this time. Just think about it," Shtock said, turning to his son, "Uncle Pavlik tells us he used to catch fish with bare hands—that's right, with his bare hands. Now that's quite a story! Listen, Pavlik, weren't you afraid of crayfish? Son, Uncle Pavlik is obviously joking. You're joking, aren't you, Pavlik?"

"So you don't believe me?" Pavel wheezed out, too tired to argue. "Still?"

The grandfather clock in the dining room struck one. Pavel got up and gently touched his wife's slender shoulder. "Shall we go, love?"

In the foyer, as they traded their thanks and good-byes, Pavel said to his host: "Come with me this summer. We'll drive to the lake, look at the old campsite, and I'll show you how to catch fish with bare hands. We can bring the girls, bring Kirill. Have a picnic, swim, kick back."

Shtock patted Pavlik on the back and kissed Alyona three times on her blanched cheeks. "Sure, sure, we'll all go, of course we will. You just say the word," he murmured as he closed the door behind them.

Poplars lining the black thoroughfare had fleshy buds. The Lidins waited for about ten minutes before finally flagging down a dirty yellow cab with a green orb in the upper left corner of its windshield. Alyona immediately fell asleep on Pavlik's shoulder. Escaping through a cracked window, her vodka breath mixed with the scents of springtime Moscow. Pavel closed his eyes. The cabby, wearing a brown faux-leather jacket over a striped navy T-shirt, studied his clients in the rearview mirror. He was bored and felt like pouring his heart out. They look like intellectuals, the cabby thought to himself, and both are drunk as skunks.

THEY HAD PASSED THE FIRST DAY raising tents and digging gutters around them, setting up a field kitchen, putting together long tables from the heavy pine boards they had brought from the city. They ate after sunset. The porridge smelled like soot, but Pavlik liked eating from a dented aluminum bowl and drinking tea with thick slices of rough bran bread. After supper, they all sat around the big fire telling stories. Although Pavlik wanted to check out the lake and surrounding forest, he couldn't just get up and leave. What would the other boys think? He didn't want to be questioned or teased. As he was falling asleep, he decided to get up at dawn and explore the campsite.

He woke up and crawled out of the tent. The sun was rising, dispersing clouds of steam that rolled over the lake's surface. The lake lay just a short distance from the tent, the shore inclined over the water like the bridge of a crooked nose. Pavlik noticed a narrow path in the reeds. He paused before setting his foot on the wet path. As soon as the sole of his right foot touched the slippery brown ground, he stepped back. Cold, slimy bottom. Snakes. Leeches. Pavlik was convulsed with disgust as he imagined stepping on the unsteady bottom with both feet. He stood there for a few minutes, then turned and walked away from the lake. He decided to try again later when the other boys were swimming.

He looked at the edge of the forest. His eyes slid across the fir treetops, then caressed the heavy lower branches. Then his eyes lingered under a birch tree, looking for slippery jacks or other early summer mushrooms. A magpie sitting atop a mossy stump caught his attention. Her wings were spread, and Pavlik was struck by the primordial whiteness of her down feathers against the black feathers of her wings and body. He tried to get closer to the magpie, but the heavy bottoms of his dew-soaked trousers rustled as they came across the bristly sedge. The magpie shuddered, now showing but a few white streaks on her tail. Pavlik attempted another step, but the magpie took off, zigzagging along the lake's shore. She was long gone from sight while Pavlik, motionless, still marveled at her beauty.

He was now facing the water, standing on the sloping shore. How about diving instead of wading into the water? Why didn't I think of that before? Pavlik leaned over the water and realized that he wouldn't be able to dive either. He was scared. He was alone at the shore. The sun was rising. There weren't even any bugs sliding over the surface of the lake. Pavlik squatted, then tried to bring his head closer to the water at different angles. Nothing helped. The same black stillness, the same reflection of his own face. Lying on the shore with his head leaning over the water, he closed his eyes for a split second. Then he looked at the horizon, at the dark green and blue coming together over the opposite shore. Ducks circled over the lake. Arrows were moving across the surface. A pike must be chasing minnows, he thought. Pavlik lowered his eyes again. A woman's face now stared at him from the black water. The face was perfectly ordinary, with freckles and gaps between the teeth. Pale blue eyes, a small mouth, a pug nose. Thin whitish lips. Little mounds of cheekbones. A regular peasant face. Only one thing was strange: lips and cheeks had a green luster, the color of lake weed. The face's small mouth opened into a smile. The corners of her eyes shook as the face laughed soundlessly. Astonished, Pavlik wanted to scream, "What?" but a hand appeared from under the black water and pressed an index finger against her lips. He couldn't move. The face smiled again, but the bugle began to play, and the camp began to move and buzz beyond Pavlik's back. He became so confused that he could only turn his head back and forth between the water and the tents, which he did until the female face disappeared below the lake's black surface.

A few days went by. Pavlik had already explored the lake shore and the adjacent forest. He sought out spots where early wild strawberries showed through the silky strings of grass. He also located three duck nests in the thick reeds of the opposite shore. He found hazelnut bushes where he expected to pick nuts toward the middle of August. He followed an old peasant woman to a distant clearing in the forest where chanterelles would later grow by the hundreds. Finally, Pavlik found a spot where a young doe came every afternoon. She bathed her elongated muzzle and small ears in the sun rays that sifted through the foliage. She would stand there, gently swaying on her thin legs. Then suddenly, as though she could hear the earth tremble under her hooves, her whole body would grow taut, like a string, and she would rush off into the thick forest. It appeared to Pavlik that she went straight through the trunks without ever shifting from a perfectly direct course.

He had done everything that country, lake, and forest had to offer, but he still hadn't swum in the lake. Remembering the face of the young woman he had seen in the water, he almost convinced himself that he had hallucinated from a lack of sleep and from blood rushing to his lowered head. He was no longer terrified of going in, but he nonetheless decided to avoid it as long as he could. Instead of washing his body in the lake like the other boys, Pavlik used a bucket, claiming he had a boil on his knee and shouldn't expose it to water. But his turn to get fish finally came, and he couldn't get out of it. It was a duty, a chore.

"Now listen here, Pavlik, watch out," the head counselor instructed him. "If you start suffocating, to hell with the fish, just drop it and get out. Understand?"

Pavlik uttered a feeble "yes," checked whether the mesh sack was properly tied to his waist, and walked toward the water. Other boys followed him with their eyes. They all had dived to get fish at one time or another already. Pavlik went slowly into the water, treading on his heels in order to minimize contact with the slimy bottom. He walked this way until the water covered his waist. He felt the surface with his palms, turned to look at the boys waiting at the shore, and then went under. He expected the fish caves to be somewhere to his left, under the high slope of the shore, and he swam in that direction with eyes closed. He opened his eyes only after his hands reached the shore's underseam. The water was clear and not black as he had expected. He half-opened his mouth and tasted clay, as though he was drinking from a mug that hadn't been fired but had dried in the sun. Piercing through a layer of lake water, the sun's rays were dark green. For a moment Pavlik lost direction as he moved across sun-striated water, but then something cold and slippery, like the back side of a kitchen knife, touched his feet. Fish, I'm supposed to catch it . . . cave. . . . He panicked at first, but pushed himself down to where he had felt the cold sensation. He noticed several openings in the shore, each a little wider than the spread of his shoulders. He stretched out his hand and felt the water pulsating under it, as though a mill was running on a nearby brook. Fish crowded inside the caves, and all he had to do now was to grab as many as he could while the air lasted in his lungs. He inserted his head and shoulders in one of the caves and saw yellow eyes and orange gills glitter in the darkness. And immediately to his left, there smiled the face of the woman he had seen on his first morning at the camp. Green dots of freckles on her chubby cheeks and on her nose. Mischievous eyes. Greenish lips, the lower protruding and the upper bitten in. Malachite hair with strands of fading yellow. The corner of the cave was dark, and Pavlik could see only the young woman's head and the outline of her neck and shoulders. At first his heart jumped up and down. He felt like shouting "help," but the face in front of him smiled so innocently and gently that instead of "help" he bubbled out: "But this can't be!"

"But I'm right here before you, which means that it is. Hello, Pavlik." The young woman's face moved closer to Pavlik's.

"How do you know my name?"

"I can hear everything you boys talk about."

"What if we get together, my friend Fedya and I, bring a huge net, and catch you?" Pavlik trilled out.

The woman's face turned sad for a moment, her eyes lost their shine, the green blush paled.

"You could never catch me anyway. But if you do try, you will never see me again. So please don't tell anybody you saw me. You promise?"

Pavlik nodded, and her face regained its disarming smile, a smile that revealed gaps between the greenish teeth. He felt that he was running out of air, but groped around, still hoping to catch fish. They were so slippery he couldn't grasp them. He pushed out and swam upward toward the green sun, propelling his legs and feet like a tail.

Jumping out of the water, Pavlik gulped some air and turned on his back. Two boys helped him onto the shore. The others surrounded him. He lay on the ground breathing heavily. Somebody unfastened the net from his waist. What do I say? I didn't catch any fish, rushed through Pavlik's head. But Fyodor Shtock, Fedya, his bosom friend since they had been in kindergarten before the war, was already shaking out the contents of Pavlik's net. Two perch pikes, two tenches, and a large catfish fell into the grass, all gasping in unison with Pavlik. It's better to leave it like this . . . , and Pavlik gave the boys a tired smile.

So this is how it happened that Pavlik started carrying a deep secret in his heart. Many times during the next three weeks he would be unable to sleep, overcome by an urge to sneak out, hide in the reeds, and wait for the lake girl to come out of the water. He was dying to find out whether she had a place on the shore, perhaps a hut in a hidden forest clearing. Or could it be that she never left her underwater cave? But each time fear and the burden of the promise he had given kept him back.

Finally, after many hours of lying awake at night, he decided to tell his friend Fedya Shtock. He just had to share his secret! Fedya was his oldest friend. Before the war and the German invasion, they used to live in the same building and had played ball and puck in the yard. Their mothers knew each other, and even their nannies came from the same area in southern Russia and used to sit on a sunlit bench in the park noshing roasted sunflower seeds, gossiping about their employers, and watching the two boys at play. During the war, while Pavlik's father was fighting the Germans at the White Sea and Fedya's father was developing new weapons at a research lab in the outskirts of Moscow, the boys and their mothers had been evacuated from Moscow. Pavlik and his mother went to the Ural region with its austere winters, while Fedya and his mother spent the first three years of the war in the warm and exotic Ashkhabad in Turkmenia. Pavlik's father was killed when a German submarine hit the torpedo boat he commanded. While Pavlik and his mother were away during the war, the family of a Moscow cop had installed itself in their rooms. When they returned to Moscow, they were given a new room in a building just a couple of blocks from the old one. By the end of the war, Fedya's father, a physicist who was of Baltic German extraction (hence the name "Shtock," which some mistook for a Jewish one), had emerged as a leading expert in what would become the Rocket Institute. For his services to the state he was given an apartment in their prewar neighborhood, and Fedya and his mother, the daughter of sculptor Klyachko, had gone to live there after they returned from Central Asia in the autumn of 1944. Although separated by the war, the two boys now ended up in the same class in middle school, and they picked up their friendship where they had left it in 1941.

After supper, as the two of them were gathering dry wood for the fire, Pavlik pulled Fedya by the sleeve of his plaid polo short.

"Swear you won't tell!"

"Tell what?"

"Just say you swear!"

"Okay, I swear," Fedya replied, folding his arms and assuming the pose of an adult who doesn't want to be bothered by a child.

"I've got a girlfriend."

"No way!"

"Three weeks today."

"From the village?"

"Well, I don't know. She may be."

"So how did you meet?"

"She lives in the lake, in a cave in the shore."

"For real?"

"Yes. For real."

"Is she a mermaid?"

"I don't know. But she's real. Like us. She can talk."

"Can I go see her?"

"No."

"Why not?"

"Because I promised."

"Promised whom? The mermaid?"

"Leave me alone, I said I promised. I promised her."

Pavlik made Fedya swear on his life, on his front teeth, and on his coin collection that he wouldn't tell another soul about Pavlik's secret meetings with the lake girlfriend. That he wouldn't try looking for her behind Pavlik's back.

Pavlik passed the rest of the summer feeling, in turn, anxiety, longing, and pride for owning an adult romantic secret. And when his turn came to get fish, he would dive in and find the cave, where a laughing green face was waiting.

"Hello, Pavlik, my sweet," she would say. "Did you miss me?"

He never knew what to answer. They would stare at each other, and then Pavlik would go up. There would always be five or six beautiful fish in his net. The other boys envied his catches. No one else brought up such pike perches shining like tinfoil, such wide golden breams, such gorgeous, long-whiskered catfish. Catfish were his favorites. After diving, the catcher was supposed to clean the fish and cut them up for chowder and frying. Pike perches were easy: he would just whack them on the head with a rock so they wouldn't jump around, remove the scales with a large spoon, then clean out the guts. Breams were a little more difficult to clean because of their width: he had to stick his fingers under the gills and hold them this way while cleaning them. As for the catfish, he always cleaned them last. They could stay alive for several hours in wet grass, breathing like grenadiers left to die on a battlefield.

On the night before their departure from the camp, boys in his tent talked about their first love adventures. Several had been seeing local village girls. They were the ones who did most of the talking. The rest nodded in approval and asked questions. Pavlik wasn't listening. His thoughts were focused on going back to Moscow, on the lake—and on the young woman's green, smiling cheeks.

"Pavlik, did you ever get laid this summer?" asked Boris Shchyukin, a stocky fellow with blond, almost colorless hair, eyelids, and eyebrows, and the arms and shoulders of a wrestler. Boris's father, a pilot, had been shot down over East Prussia. Boris and Pavlik had in common their fathers' valor and death, so Pavlik hadn't expected Boris to put him on the spot like that. But Boris was one of those sharp-tongued and unpredictable characters who live to win by hook or crook, know no loyalties, and like to speak in the name of the collective.

"So, did you?" Boris asked.

Pavlik didn't answer.

"Come on, we're all buddies here," Boris pressed on, a twisted smile on his lips. "Your friend Fedya told us you've been having fun with some chick in the lake."

"What're you talking about?" Pavlik mumbled, turning his head toward Fedya and not finding him in his sleeping bag. "How could he!" rushed through Pavlik's head. He looked at the boys' expectant faces, lit by a kerosene lamp known as "the bat."

Pavlik licked his lips. "What do you all care? I've been doing it with a mermaid in the lake every day. I've done it more than all of you here. Just leave me alone." He turned away and hid his face in the pillow.

"A mermaid? What a bunch of crap," someone said, but the others hushed him down, either because they now revered Pavlik even more or because they didn't want to tease an angry dog.

Pavlik was grim the next morning. He silently accepted the Best Catch Prize from the head counselor; he then got onto a bus and toppled down on the backseat. The buses drove through the village that flanked the highway. The villagers, mostly women in floral shawls and ragged children, stood in front of the huts and waved their hands. The boys on the bus waved back and made goofy faces. When his bus passed the last house on the edge of the village, Pavlik put his head to the window. From the house's porch a pair of familiar green eyes shot up at him. He pressed the bridge of his nose and his lips to glass that was smeared with August mud and watched the green silhouette melt into the background.

After their return to Moscow, Pavlik didn't speak to Fedya Shtock for almost two years. Fedya tried to regain his friendship a number of times, coming up to Pavlik during intercessions and at the cafeteria, sending classmates as messengers, writing apologetic notes and leaving them on Pavlik's desk in the classroom. Once he came over after school with his coin collection as a peace offering, but Pavlik told him to "go to weasel hell." But teenage memory eventually forgives even what it doesn't forget, and in junior high school Pavlik and Fedya found themselves first on barely speaking terms and then increasingly friendly again, especially since they were now members of a circle of children of the intelligentsia, many of whom felt especially vulnerable in those anticosmopolitan times.

And then they both fell in love with Alyona Tarsis in the summer after ninth grade. Alyona was unlike all her peers in the all-girl high school where boys from their school were sometimes invited to dances and socials. She was different. She had blazing red hair and an inimitable smile. She carried about her an air that words could not describe: both summery and wintry, hot and cold, like the scent of a ripe cranberry unpicked and frozen on a bog. She had the tightest skirts of any girl they knew. Her weightless feet glided, not walked. She became—was—the girl of their dreams.

Alyona shared a tiny room in a communal apartment with her mother, an actress at the Stanislavsky Theater. The mother, Jadviga, was Polish, a leggy blonde with bloodshot, pale blue eyes. She was always dressed in black or mousy gray; her sibilants were screechy and hissy to a Russian ear. Before his arrest and death in a labor camp at Kolyma, Alyona's father, Itsik Tarsis, had been a professor of Yiddish at the Pedagogical Institute. He had published several books and a Yiddish-Russian dictionary. Pavlik found the story of Alyona's father particularly beguiling and even went so far as to compare it in his mind with the lot of his own Jewish father, a war hero who had been killed fighting the Germans.

Pavlik's mother, Ida Ruvimovna, a gynecologist who worked in a clinic at one of Moscow's largest factories and had seen it all, was not keen on Alyona. "She is from the wrong family," was the verdict she gave Pavlik after Alyona had been to their house for supper.

"But, mother, her father was a professor, her mother's an actress. How much better does it get?"

"Poles are anti-Semites, don't you know that?"

"But her father was Jewish and a linguist."

"Well, he chose the wrong language, didn't he?" Pavlik's mother said under her breath. "In any case, she's no good, this girl, she's trouble."

Unlike his friend Pavlik Lidin, who was always direct and help-lessly honest, Fedya Shtock had been, even back then, a master of embellishment, a wizard of concealment. With a few strokes of fancy he transformed Alyona's father into a military officer who had shared the wartime fate of Pavlik's father and the fathers of a few other class-mates. Fedya's parents liked the fact that Alyona's mother came from the *szlachta*—the Polish gentry. "She's very good-looking. A true Polish beauty. Blue blood!" Fedya's mother said after meeting Alyona for the first time. Fedya's father, the rocket scientist, was almost never home in those days, and his mother was her son's adviser on matters ranging from flowers for a date to shaving cream.

By the winter of their tenth and last year of secondary school, Alyona and Fedya had become a steady couple. Everyone expected that they would get married after graduation. Pavlik remained close to both, offering Alyona if not love, then his brotherly protection. He had a local reputation as a fearless fighter and defender of children, many of them the bespectacled and violin-carrying Jewish boys and girls, from bullies and bigots. To Fedya, he could offer, among many other gifts, the comfort of knowing that Pavlik would never betray him. Never, under any circumstances. There was something courtly in Pavlik's friendship with Alyona and Fedya. Pavlik could act nobly toward his rival while also dying of love for Alyona. Fedya sensed his friend's chivalric quality right away and put it to personal use. Pavlik gave him the keys to his room for afternoon rendezvous, and Fedya and Alyona would cut school and spend time there alone while Pavlik's mother was at the clinic. Pavlik helped Fedya punish an obnoxious fellow from Alyona's building who once tried to grab her in a dark archway—or, rather, Pavlik did the beating while Fedya stood by in his clean clothes, looking like a referee at a boxing match. And it was Pavlik to whom Fedya turned for help when he got Alyona pregnant.

It was, of all dates, April 1, and Pavlik didn't believe him right away.

"Alyona's pregnant? Very funny. And I've been accepted to Moscow University."

They were standing outside Pavlik's apartment, its door covered with many layers of maroon paint. On the frame were doorbells of various sizes and shapes for the seven families that inhabited this communal labyrinth.

"Pavlik, I mean it. She thinks she's almost three months' pregnant. What am I going to do?" Fedya looked scared; he was twitching his fingers, something Pavlik knew he did only when he was extremely agitated.

"Come in, don't stand in the doorway," Pavlik led Fedya into the long, narrow room he shared with his mother. "So she's pregnant. Congratulations! You can name the son after me. Do you want to eat something?"

"What? No, nothing for me," Fedya replied. "What was she thinking? I don't know what to do now."

"What to do? Nothing. You'll just get married a little earlier, that's all." Pavlik sounded almost relieved that these months of uncertainty had come to an end.

"Married? A joke, right?" Fedya sprang up from his chair. "I cannot marry her. What are we going to do—get married and have a baby? Be a goddamn young Soviet family? I've got to go to university, then to graduate school. I've got plans for my life, as do you, don't you? What's the matter, Pavlik?"

With his right hand Pavlik grabbed Fedya by the front of his striped blue shirt at his throat. "Get out of my house before I put your ass where your face is." Pavlik's face turned crimson as he dragged Fedya through the long communal corridor.

"Pavlik, wait, you're overreacting. We're friends, we tell each other everything. Please . . . "

"I never want to see you again, you . . . you scum." Pavlik pushed Fedya out the door and slammed it.

He went to the bathroom and sat there for a while, smoking the *papirosy* that he kept hidden behind the main water pipe. Then he put on a coat made from his father's old navy uniform and went outside. He wandered the wet streets until dark, taking in the fumes and smells of vernal Moscow and trying to calm down. When he came home, he found Alyona sitting on his bed; she was sipping tea from a faceted glass and quietly weeping, weeping and shaking. Next to her on the bed sat Pavlik's mother in a dark green dress with a brooch on her large chest. She had one of her arms over Alyona and was slowly stroking the girl's back and nape. "My poor girl," Pavlik's mother kept whispering. "All will be well, trust me."

When all this happened, Alyona's mother was away on a tour with a group of actors in her theater company. Pavlik's mother, who had had a quick change of heart toward Alyona, helped her get an abortion at the factory clinic. The rest of what happened followed suit. Alyona flunked most of her graduation exams and didn't get her high school diploma that year. Pavlik applied to Moscow University to study physics but didn't get in; the year was 1950. For the next five years he studied at the Institute of Transportation—joining the ranks of the many unwilling Jewish Soviet engineers in training. Several nights a week he unloaded freight trains to support himself and Alyona, whom he had married. They were childless—one of the many results of Alyona's abortion. Another was her depression. Fedya Shtock, who eventually slithered his way back into their lives, studied ethnography at Moscow University. He married late, when he was already in graduate school. His wife, who had gone to high school with Alyona, was the daughter of an air force general. . . .

Pavel Lidin remembered and relived all this—the older he was in the recollections, the faster the clip—as he was riding in the taxi-cab that wet April night in Moscow. During the ride he kept his eyes closed and warmed with his hands and lips the bloodless fingers of his sleeping wife.

WHEN SUMMER CAME, Pavel and Alyona Lidin went on their annual beach vacation to Palanga, Lithuania. Fyodor Shtock, his wife, and their son Kirill also went away, to the Black Sea resort of Pitsunda. Pavel's account of fishing in '45 would have been for-gotten—just as were many of Pavel's other stories—had it not been for Kirill. He kept nudging his skeptical father with questions. For a while Shtock ignored him, but Kirill persisted with a teenager's loyalty to wondrous memories.

"Papa, why can't we go to Uncle Pavlik's lake? What if Uncle Pavlik wasn't joking about catching fish with his bare hands? Papa? Can we please go?"

Shtock considered his son's request and agreed to go to the lake after their return to Moscow, hoping that Kirill would forget this promise by the end of the summer. But Kirill didn't forget, so Shtock had no choice.

Pavel had gotten back from his vacation just a few days earlier. Shtock's call surprised and alarmed him. What if there are no more fish? What then? Shtock will tease me for months after. But I didn't call him, he called me. It's he who's curious. And what if there's still plenty of fish in the lake? I should be able to catch some, Pavel mused after talking with Shtock.

Shtock's wife never went to the country; she said she despised "sylvan pleasures." Alyona wanted to come along but—in a show of female solidarity—ended up staying behind to keep her company. They went in Shtock's car. Kirill slept on the backseat while Pavel and Shtock chatted quietly. They drove for more than an hour before turning off the highway at Novopetrovskoe.

"The village should be about half a mile from here," Pavel indicated the direction with his hand.

A single log cabin had survived on the edge of the village; its roof was about to fall in. Where other houses had once stood now grew elder bushes and tall grass. Plants of desolation—rosebay, darnel, and fescue—now ruled over the empty space.

"My God, there's nothing left!" Pavel cried out.

"I hope the lake is still there at least," Shtock felt irritation stirring in his stomach.

At that point Kirill woke up and shouted: "Papa, papa, the lake!"

And they drove out onto the shore.

The forest had moved even closer to the water. The lake's dark surface glistened like an amethyst set in blackened silver.

By late afternoon they had eaten all their picnic supplies and done enough hunting for mushrooms in the forest and playing volleyball and badminton. Shtock caught a good-size pike using his fancy Swedish rod and reel, and was very proud of himself.

"Well, boys, we've got to get moving," Shtock said and looked at his watch. "Go ahead, Pavlik, and dive in. Show us how you do it, and we'll head back." He was waiting for Pavel to make a fool of himself. "The old girls must be tired of keeping our dinner warm. I don't know about you, but I'm starving."

Shtock held a double towel for Pavel. I bet he'll come out after thirty seconds with the excuse that the water is too cold, he thought to himself.

Pavel undressed and placed his watch atop the pile of clothes. He removed a leather belt from his jeans, put it around his waist and attached a mesh sack.

"Well, guys, wait for the catch," Pavel said as he walked to the water.

He dove with a splash and swiftly took to the left, going under the sloping high shore. His hands didn't fail to find the cave. He stretched out a hand, then another, then thrust his head into the cave. A few scared fish dashed past him. Their cold tails touched his hips. Damn, it's cold, he thought as he turned his head to the right. From the cave's right corner an old woman was staring at him. Pavel shivered, so repulsive was her face. Her skin resembled a toad's: dark green with brown specks, all covered with folds, growths, and wrinkles. Her little eyes, set deeply in their narrow black slits, were colorless. Her lips were nearly gone; a toothless, slimy mouth surrounded a gaping hole between a bulbous nose and a receding chin.

Pavel slowly began to retreat away from the corner, although he still couldn't tear his eyes away from the old woman's face.

"Pavlik, honey, you're back," and some semblance of a smile formed out of the folds. The old woman's wrinkly hand now reached out to feel Pavlik's cheek.

"A-a-a-ah!!!" Pavel pulled back as if losing strength.

Coming out of the water, Pavel saw that Shtock had undressed to dive in for rescue. Pavel walked onto the shore and past Shtock toward his clothes. Everything went blurry, and he fell on the ground. Having come to, he saw that Shtock was fussing about him, rubbing his chest and temples.

Shtock sounded genuinely worried: "Look, Pavlik, you're not a kid, you can't risk your life like this. What if something had happened underwater?"

"How . . . "

But Shtock interrupted Pavel. "Who needs the stupid fish! What if your heart had failed?"

Shtock looked at Kirill, who at that moment was spreading out the catch on the grass—two pike perches, two tenches, and a catfish. Kirill stared at the fish with adoration.

"Pavlik, I have to admit," Shtock said, "I didn't think you'd catch anything. Those fish look spectacular."

Pavel lifted his eyes to Shtock. "I'm an old man! How long ago this must have been. I'm old! Dear God!" He rolled over, lay his head on the ground and started to weep, rubbing his cheeks against blades of grass.

"Come now, pal." Shtock squatted next to Pavel and put his hand on Pavel's shoulder while looking at his son with an air of incomprehension.

"Leave me alone, you don't understand!" Pavel groaned. "God, how could I have grown so old?"

All the way home in the car Pavel was sullen and grim, watching the landscape and smoking *papirosy* that came from a box with a picture of the White Sea Canal. It wasn't until later, at the Shtocks', after a few drinks and a supper of fried fish and potatoes with mushrooms and onions, that he relaxed and mellowed, starting to resemble his usual self.

When Kirill went to bed, the two men and their wives moved to the living room. Over coffee with liqueurs, Shtock treated them to the latest round of gossip from the Research Institute of Anthropology. Pavel occasionally uttered a few words, more often something like "uh-hum." He held before his eyes a green faceted tumbler with a splash of orange liqueur at the bottom.

"So here we are, you, Alyona, and I," Shtock said after he refreshed their drinks. "We've known each other our whole lives, since we were children, right?" Nodding as he spoke, he turned his eyes to Alyona, then to Pavel, then to his wife. "So I thought I'd propose a little toast to our friendship, to having stuck together. To friendship!"

Shtock raised his tumbler, brought it to his wife's and let it clink, then did the same with Alyona's. He moved his hand with the tumbler toward Pavel, but Pavel didn't move.

"Pavlik, let's chin-chin, old fellow. To our long friendship!"

Pavel wasn't listening. He turned the tumbler very slowly between three fingers while pointing it to different pieces of furniture: a divan, an armchair, a bookcase, a lamp. He then aimed the glass at his wife, who was sitting, her legs folded beneath her, in a velour chair. The laughing face of a young woman appeared in the green darkness of the living room. Pavel turned the tumbler again, and the shriveled face of an elderly mermaid looked at him with silent reproach. He squeezed the tumbler until the old woman's features broke into countless green slivers.

Last August in Biarritz

WAS IT THE BLINDING LIGHT coming through the gray clouds or the shrieks of the black squirrels crisscrossing the paths of Blackmoor Park? Felix Sokolovitch suddenly felt anxiety, bitter like the heart of an apricot stone. Moreover, hard as he tried, he just couldn't recall any names—people, streets, anything—from his prewar life. Surprised and bewildered, his old aunt fingered her purple moire hat. It was a Sunday in the beginning of March 1990, and Sokolovitch and his aunt were taking their noontime walk. This walk was one of the few habits to have survived from Sokolovitch's Parisian childhood and adolescence, which had been interrupted by the war, the German invasion, and their escape to America.

The air was warm and springlike, and those out walking wore light overcoats or no coats at all. Dressed in overalls and rain jackets, children ran up and down the wet, muddy park alleys, chasing the squirrels, who were mad with spring fever. Sokolovitch and his aunt stood out against the background of the old parkscape like quaint objects, a cast-iron gate or a dilapidated bench where a president once proposed to his future wife.

Sokolovitch wore an old-fashioned navy trench coat. The belt was missing; the large collar lay on his shoulders like the wings of a dead bird. Under the coat were a bluish gray tweed jacket, baggy black trousers, and a white oxford with a bumble-bee bow tie. Walking heavily, he steeped his black loafers in the mud. His right hand clasped a cane's hand-carved handle. Sokolovitch had very big hands the color of drying clay, a biblical face with a distinguished nose, a tall forehead, sarcastic nostrils, and a sharp chin projecting confidence.

In Paris before the war, Sokolovitch's unmarried aunt used to take her nephew to the Luxembourg Gardens on Sundays, while his parents were alone in their apartment on rue des Marroniers. Now his parents were long dead, and his aunt still single. When they all had sailed from Normandy in 1940, her fiancé had stayed behind, hoping to wrap up his publishing enterprise and follow them to New York. Three years later he died of inanition in a transit camp. So now, for many years, Sokolovitch had brought his aunt from Manhattan to Blackmoor on Sunday mornings. She had worked at one of the libraries of Columbia University for thirty years and now passed the remainder of her days in a rent-controlled apartment on the Upper West Side. The two of them would walk in the park together, usually reminiscing about Sokolovitch's late mother and father, the journey from Les Havres to the New World, Parisian theaters, and the quays of the Seine. The aunt's senility, spreading like a forest fire during a drought, had long been troubling Sokolovitch, but he didn't have the heart to discontinue their ritual Sunday walks.

He straightened his heavy, gold-rimmed glasses, looked at his wristwatch, and suggested that they turn in the direction of home. His wife was waiting with dinner. On Sundays they ate early, European style.

"Felix dear, last week you were telling me that very few students signed up for your seminar," the aunt asked on their way back. "I can't imagine that these young people have no interest in the history of our civilization!"

The aunt had preserved her old-time St. Petersburg accent. She would address Sokolovitch in Russian; he would answer in French. French, not Russian, was for him a truly native tongue. Born in Paris to an eye doctor's family, Sokolovitch as a child had turned away from everything Russian, replete with fading memories and chameleon longing. Besides, all those melodic miles of Corneille and

Racine he was made to memorize at the Lycée Janson de Sailly had ousted the sonorous Russian poems his mother used to recite at the tea table. Acknowledging the meaning of Russian words was a mere habit for Sokolovitch; following his parents' deaths, he completely ceased speaking Russian. At Blackmoor College, where Sokolovitch taught Latin and Greek, a newcomer would be treated to a joke, something to the effect that Professor Sokolovitch had an accent in all languages, an echo of Russian in his French, flourishes of French consonants in his Russian, and both Russian and French cadences in his otherwise flawless English.

Sokolovitch had settled down in a Colonial on Castle Street in the early 1950s, when as a young assistant professor he had moved from New York City to Long Island to teach at Blackmoor. His first wife, a Jewish-Russian émigré also formerly of Paris, had died in 1980, leaving him and their two children. Sokolovitch's daughter, now in her late thirties and married, was living in California. They didn't see each other very often. A thirty-five-year-old son stayed close to his father. For three years following his wife's death, Sokolovitch had lived a widower in his lifeless house. Then he remarried. His new wife was a genuine American. They had met in a clinic where Sally worked as a nurse and Sokolovitch was seeing a neurologist for a wartime injury to the spine that still caused a great deal of pain. Sally was plump and Irish, all laughs and merriment, Sokolovitch's junior by twelve years. They were married under a chuppah (Sally's idea) three months after they met. They renovated the Colonial and started a new life together, a life without rummaging through each other's past. The aunt, Sokolovitch's only living relative, and therefore a virtual parent to him, never got over her nephew's choice. "Sally, such a sallow name," she thought to herself in Russian ("Salli, etakoe sal'noe imia"). Naturally, she never said anything to her nephew.

At dinner, they turned again to Sokolovitch's position at Blackmoor College. He had for several years been talking of retirement.

His colleagues in the department whispered behind his back; Sokolovitch was to them as ancient as the subjects he taught. It was also the case that since the death of his first wife, he hadn't written or published a single line. At first, for about a year, he lay on the couch in a state of black melancholy. Later, after having resumed teaching, he no longer had the drive to invite his students over for a Thursday social. He tried it a few times, but his heart pounded like a netted trout when, on his request, one of his female students brought in a copper tray with tea and cakes. He felt lonely at colleagues' dinner parties and kept quiet, digging his head in randomly opened pages. The second wife never became part of her husband's university circle. An unspoken agreement between Sokolovitch and Sally marked out the boundaries of what they would and wouldn't do as a couple. Sally loved the outdoors, and they began to frequent the parks and beaches in the area, taking long walks along the coast, deserted and especially scenic from the fall until the middle of the spring.

In the early 1960s Sokolovitch had published *The Novel in Antiquity*, a book that had made him famous in the field. Unexpectedly for many, he refuted the ideas of Ian Trott, who in an influential book had linked the origins of the English novel (and the novel in general) to a particular set of socioeconomic conditions. Sokolovitch's book startled many North American literary scholars. At the crest of his success, he was made full professor. He had since been teaching mostly senior seminars, once very successful with Blackmoor students. But times were different, and so were popular teachers. For several years now Sokolovitch could barely gather three or four students into the classics seminar room . . .

"Believe it or not, I'm beginning to resemble the title character in that novel by our famous compatriot," Sokolovitch said to his aunt before gulping his strong after-dinner coffee. "Imagine, *ma tante*, I've got only one student in my seminar. They even considered canceling the class. I suppose they took pity on my old age and gray hair."

"What's he like?" Sally asked, shaking the ruffles on her chin and saggy neck.

"He who?"

"That one student?"

"Oh, actually it's a she. And I don't have much to say after two classes. She seems to listen and take notes. The other day I lectured to her about *The Golden Ass*."

They sat in the living room for another half-hour, Sokolovitch smoking and leafing through the book reviews, the women watching television until it was time to take the aunt back to Manhattan.

They didn't speak for most of the drive. A few blocks from her building, the aunt recalled a robbery in his parents' Parisian apartment in the 1930s, when Felix was away at summer camp in Brittany.

"I've been meaning to ask you, Felenka, do you remember the Vernakoff family?" she asked as Sokolovitch parked the car.

"Not really, *ma tante*," he muttered back.

"Oh, but you must remember them." The old lady suddenly became animated. "They had a girl your age, Lise, Lisotchka. The two of you went to birthday parties and the Louvre together. They got stuck in Morocco and returned to Paris only in '49."

Sokolovitch was beginning to get restless and looked at his aunt, who was moved by her own recollection. All he wanted now was to drive back home and smoke a long pipe in his den. The aunt didn't notice his inattention.

"So I heard that Lise Vernakoff killed herself in Biarritz last August. She must have been at least a year younger than you. A young woman. Isn't this just awful?"

"I'm sixty-seven, *ma tante*."

"Remember to call me when you get home, Felenka."

ON TUESDAY, the only student in Sokolovitch's seminar was late to class. Sokolovitch kept looking at the wry face of the wall clock.

Atop the pile on the table in front of him, the cover of an art book featured an erotic dance from a Greek amphora. He couldn't abide tardiness. His fingers were knocking out an impatient tango on the amphora. Finally, ten minutes later, the door was flung open. His student, Liz Linore, walked in, out of breath.

"I'm so sorry, Professor." Sokolovitch silently pointed to a chair on his left.

"It doesn't really matter, Ms. Linore," he said slowly. "This appears to be my last seminar. I've decided to retire. As of next September. Actually, I didn't just decide suddenly. I'd been carrying this idea for some time now. But today, now, I feel with such certainty that my teaching career has come to naught."

"But, Professor . . . but, Felix . . . "—excited, she called him by his first name—"you're so well known as a scholar, what about all your books and . . . your former students?"

"All those things are in the past. They all have had the pleasure of becoming history."

For a minute they stared at each other silently. Liz was still trying to catch her breath, and Sokolovitch flared his nostrils to take in her flowery perfume. The odor took him back fifty years, to someone he had once known in Paris. A memory as slender as a distant trill in the treetops. Chasing away the recollection, he slowly nodded, looking at the white lacy strap that showed from under his student's blouse. An off-white blouse with an embroidered front, a lacy shoulder strap, a cheap turquoise ring and matching earrings, a faded woven bracelet. Long auburn hair falling behind her back, flushed cheeks with dimples, an olive glare in her eyes. The old professor sank the book with the erotic amphora in his spacious briefcase and heaved his heavy frame out of the wooden swivel chair.

"Class is canceled for today. The two of us are likely to benefit from a stroll around campus before having lunch at the French bakery café. We should feel lucky there is one in our neck of the woods."

A quarter of an hour later the teacher and his student were sitting down at his favorite table at La Baguetterie, where Sokolovitch was known simply as "Professor." They both ordered baguette sandwiches with turkey and brie.

"There isn't much to tell, really," Liz was saying. "My mom came from the Appalachian Mountains. A small mining town. Everyone in her community was related. Folks in neighboring towns were wary of them. And all because of the unusual shade of their skin."

"Skin?"

"Yes. I know it's hard to imagine. Mom died when I was little. I don't remember much of her, but I do remember her hands and neck—they were a milky blue color. It almost seems to me now that a warm radiance came from her. At home we never speak of mom's origins. My dad probably still thinks that her family had some kind of a curse. You know, it was by pure chance how they met. He'd just finished military service and had no idea where to go. He stopped for a few days in mom's hometown. My elder brother came of it. My brothers take after our father."

"What does he do?" Sokolovitch asked politely.

"My dad owns a business in town, a small pickling factory. My grandfather started it. My brothers work with my dad. The younger one runs distribution and sales, the older one drives the delivery truck."

For a moment Sokolovitch shuddered, envisioning this pickled family and failing to picture Liz in their midst. But then she smiled—a mixture of irony and guilt—and that interrupted his absence.

"What about your children, Professor—I mean, Felix? I heard you have two?"

Sokolovitch took a sip of coffee, flagged down the owner to ask for a refill, wiped his glasses with a checkered handkerchief, and began to talk. From his rambling account, Liz found out about his sick boy, the thirty-five-year-old Alex. For many years Alex had been secluded in an institution ten miles west of Blackmoor. Ever since he was a small boy, he had suffered from a chronic disorder that still defied precise scientific explanation. Only the boy's late mother, Sokolovitch's first wife, could occasionally enter the corridors of her son's world, all shadows and cobwebs.

The afternoon sun had already rolled under the counter of the French bakery-café when Sokolovitch and Liz said good-bye. A purple backpack bobbing behind her, she walked in the direction of the campus. Briefcase under armpit and a bag with croissants for breakfast in hand, he headed down a wet alley toward his home.

THEY DIDN'T SEE EACH OTHER for a week. Liz arrived at class early and was already waiting in the seminar room when Sokolovitch came in, shuffling his feet. This time he lectured for more than an hour, mainly about *The Satyricon*. He barely lifted his leaden eyes from his wide palms, spread in front of him on the table like the pages of an old prayer book. He finished talking and arranged a smile on his face. He had been waiting for this moment since the previous week, both hoping and fearful to hope.

"We still have another hour to go, don't we, Liz?"

"Yes, Professor."

"Well, I was thinking . . . you don't suppose we could take a drive to the ocean? The beach is so lovely and free of bodies this time of the year. Plus, all sorts of odd objects get washed ashore. So, perhaps, the two of us can take a walk. But you must be . . . "

Liz approached his side of the long oak table.

"That sounds wonderful, Professor."

"Really?" Sokolovitch laughed to mask his embarrassment.

"Yes, really. Deserted beach, washed-up treasures. Yes, all this sounds wonderful! I'd love to go."

Half an hour later they were furrowing the damp sand. Frostbitten crab shells rustled under their feet. Liz stopped frequently to pick up a round, ocean-polished piece of pink quartz or a black pebble with a sparkling streak of mica. When they had walked for a while, they turned and looked back. The dunes. The wilted rushes. The cold shine of his Buick in the distant parking lot. And the rattle of the scenic road. Liz ran up to the top of a dune. Dazzled by her grace, Sokolovitch stood motionless. Was he thinking, during their first walk on the beach, that in this sunlit haven of seagulls and sand-pipers, on these spring sand dunes, danced his last love?

A seagull's wing nearly hit the bridge of his nose. Sokolovitch swallowed a gulp of salty air. It felt like a spasm in his chest: *mm-umm-mm*. Liz ran up to him.

"Felix, what's the matter?"

"Just something in my eye. Probably a sand particle. I'm fine."

"Let me look. Lift up your eyelid."

"It's fine now. Perhaps just the wind."

"You're sure?"

"Perhaps it's too early to open the beach season. Look, all the seagulls are going someplace. How they scream. . . . You're probably hungry, dear Liz. How about lunch? There's a decent restaurant nearby."

He had washed his face and hands in the restaurant bathroom. Looking at himself in the grimy mirror, Sokolovitch realized that he wouldn't have the fervor to take her hand in the car or to kiss her.

He wanted to talk to Liz right there, in the half-empty restaurant—to set a formal tone for their subsequent meetings. But Liz looked so happy, sipping lemonade from a dark blue glass. She smiled at her frazzled companion with such ease that he only sighed, sat down at the table, and emptied a packet of sweetener into his coffee mug.

ON FRIDAYS every other week Sokolovitch visited his son at the institution. In the family circle, *the home* had been the preferred term for this place. Sally never came along with him. It was all part of their arrangement. On a visiting Friday, Sokolovitch would have a bite to eat in a Greek place near the campus before driving to "the home."

Grilled lamb. Soft pita bread. Tomatoes and sprigs of parsley. Yogurt sauce with cucumbers. Coffee out of a paper cup. Heracles running. Sokolovitch liked to address the owner, Mikis, in classical Greek. Shaving off curls of lamb with a long, crooked knife, Mikis smiled at the words he vaguely remembered from school and responded in the language of Heracles' modern heirs.

But this time Sokolovitch was in too much of a hurry. He couldn't allow himself the pleasure of relishing his food, of slowly blending in his mouth the spicy warmth and the sour coolness, chewy lamb and tender tomato flesh. He swallowed his lunch, placed six dollars and a handful of change on the counter, and walked out with a paper cup in hand, spilling coffee on the steps and his black loafers.

Five minutes later, his PhotoGray lenses already swelling with darkness, Sokolovitch stopped his car across the street from the old clock tower on the eastern corner of the college green. Liz was already there, waiting: a shepherd's canvas sack with a long strap, jeans held on her hips by a thick leather belt, a velvet ribbon in her hair, a white shirt, a black denim jacket.

"It's not too late to turn around," Sokolovitch said after they left Blackmoor behind. "I think it might be better if I went alone."

"Felix, I want to see him. For myself. And for you. I want to be able to understand. Please let me come with you. And also, didn't you say that since . . . that no one there treats him like a mother . . . ?"

They drove along the coast, passing empty beaches—still home to birds alone.

"Can we roll the windows down? I want to feel the breeze. Do you mind, Felix?"

The professor mechanically pressed his finger to the cold button on the door. The car filled with the smells of rotten fish, seaweed, and spring rain. The road went down at a steep angle, then leaped up and started winding. To the right of the highway, on a hill amid elms and poplars, there stood a turreted sage green Victorian with purple trim and yellow accents. They parked in front of its gates, climbed up to the entrance, and now stood there shuffling their feet, both of them uneasy with anticipation.

To Sokolovitch's great surprise, the visit started off quite well. Alex immediately took to Liz. His grimaces, gawky motions, and asymmetrical smiles—usually painful to watch—now indicated sprouting thoughts, caricatures of emotions, shadows of recognition. This boy-man jumped around Liz, who fed him strawberries. He touched her hands and neck. He clapped his hands with their long fingers and perfect nails. Sokolovitch stayed with his son longer than usual. Then he went out to the lobby to smoke his pipe. Liz remained in the room with Alex.

After a rendezvous with aromatic tobacco, Sokolovitch knocked the ashes out of the pipe into a marble ashtray and lifted himself from a deep leather sofa. He was now ready to leave.

"Well, son, it's time for us to be going." Sokolovitch reached out his right hand to pet his son on the cheek. "Liz has to go back to work. Don't you, Liz?"

"Look at him," Liz whispered. "Look, he's smiling. He's happy."

"Liz, we must be going. This has been a long visit." Sokolovitch sounded unexpectedly firm.

At this point Alex started squealing and whining. First, he sat down on the carpet, pounding the floor with clenched fists. Then he tried to get up, but stepped on his long pants and fell. He hit an elbow and began shaking with anger and turning white. His glassy eyes went back and forth between his father and Liz.

Sokolovitch towered in the middle of the room, hands buried in the stretched pockets of his navy pants, eyes chained to his son's convulsing body. For a minute his son grew quiet; his face assumed a serene expression. Gray-green intelligent eyes. Hawk nose. Thick, jet black hair. High forehead. Then he started beating his head against the floor. It was a particularly bad outburst.

When the orderlies, summoned by Liz, ran into the room, the faces of both father and son showed terror. The son's terror came from an instinctual fear of punishment, the father's from having just realized that in that brief moment of quiet his insane son had looked exactly like him, Felix Sokolovitch, in a wartime photograph. Sokolovitch had had the photograph taken in the Philippines and sent to his parents in New York. He had just come out of the hospital after a spine injury. Poor girl, Sokolovitch thought. What must she be thinking after all this? Especially when the resemblance between us must be so apparent. It's like seeing myself forty-five years back. And next to that younger me is an old wreck, the present me. This is like a separation of body and soul. My present-day soul, the soul of Felix Sokolovitch, a professor of classics, one foot in the grave, and this young body, my young body, my son's . . .

The heavy door with its stained-glass panel slammed shut after the attendant let them out of "the home." The professor and his student didn't speak until they reached the outskirts of Blackmoor.

It had usually been the case that after a stroll on the beach or a cup of coffee at the French bakery-café, Sokolovitch would take Liz back to the main campus parking lot, where they would part. This time, lost in his thoughts about their imminent separation, break-up, or good-bye, Sokolovitch turned the wrong way at the light, heading toward the area of Blackmoor where shopkeepers and tradesmen had traditionally owned homes.

"Could you stop the car? That's my house over there."

Sokolovitch hit the brakes.

"I wish you'd listened to me and never come along," he said, mournfully.

His silver Buick pulled over, and Liz stood on the sidewalk in front of her house, listening to the rustle of the naked weeping

willows. A big, greasy dog ran out to greet her. She dropped her
backpack on the screened porch and went inside.

LIZ'S MOTHER had died young, so Liz had grown up in a house
with three males. For a few years her father's unmarried sister had
looked after the kids. When Liz was in high school, an old woman
by the name of Sabina, a refugee from someplace in eastern Europe,
had taken over the cooking and cleaning. The old woman slept in
the basement amid three old bicycles, a washer and dryer, and all
sorts of junk. Liz's father and unmarried brothers, all three having
barely earned their high school diplomas, regarded her college studies with workingmen's distrust of abstract knowledge.

During her first two years at Blackmoor College, Liz had lived
in a dormitory, although the campus was no more than a fifteen-
minute walk away from her home. After her sophomore year, though,
she moved back home. But she was never there during the day. She
stayed on campus until late, reading at the library, and came home
when the men were already asleep. Their day started at five in the
morning with a breakfast at a diner. Liz would usually learn about
family news from the old housekeeper, who made her breakfast and
waited to heat up her dinner at night.

After Liz and Sokolovitch started spending time together, she
grew even more indifferent toward her family. She would never
have expected that for some time now her father and brother had
known about her off-campus dates with Sokolovitch and had been
following her around. It all had started with a foreign and therefore
suspicious name. Once or twice during a rare family breakfast or
dinner on the weekend Liz had mentioned her "wonderful and brilliant" classics professor. She was so convinced that her father and
brothers wouldn't make anything of her fondness—either for Latin
prose or for the old émigré professor—that she didn't even think
to be circumspect. Blackmoor was, however, a small town, and the

owner of La Baguetterie happened to be her father's occasional hunting partner. Over a drink, the baker had told her father about a "pretty girl" who had been frequenting his place in the company of the "professor."

"We think that their kind rot in libraries. We figure these guys don't have a life, just books and papers. But what do you know: our professor brings a female student for a cup of coffee and pastry. Real cute, long hair, the works. . . . And the way she stares at him! The old prof has the girl totally in love."

Something screeched inside the father's head like a rusty gear.

"Bullshit," he barked at the baker. "Why would she go with an old man?"

"Look, buddy, I'm telling you, those young girls have the hots for professor types," the baker pushed on. "By the way, when's your daughter graduating?"

"Supposed to finish this year."

"That's good. At least you'll have someone with a college degree in the family business."

After talking with the baker, Liz's father tossed in bed, unable to sleep. He recalled, in turn, his dead wife at the maternity ward and Liz as a little girl in a purple gauze tutu at a ballet recital. He got up to smoke on the porch. Giving forth short puffs of smoke, like a firing revolver, he picked up Liz's backpack from the floor. One by one, his pickled hands removed books and notebooks from the backpack. Breathing raggedly, he flipped through the pages of a book whose title he couldn't understand, except that the author had a long, foreign name. Then he turned to the inner flap with the picture of a bearded and bespectacled face, and the accompanying words "professor" and "Blackmoor College." He didn't sleep the rest of the night.

In the morning he got up furious, determined to track the professor down and protect his daughter. At breakfast— muddy coffee with oily doughnuts—the father told his sons of his discovery. They ruled out any official channels, convinced that all foreigners

and university rats in glasses and tweeds were part of a conspiracy
against the common man. They decided to wait and follow Liz
around. They were most in favor of a quiet punishment. A metal
pipe or a chain would do.

"Wait, why don't we talk to her first?" the younger brother tried
to caution his father and sibling. "What if we get in trouble?"

"Feeling sorry for the old bastard? Look at him, he feels sorry,"
the older brother raged. "You think the prof ever felt sorry for
Lizzie?"

"It's a friggin' disgrace!" added Liz's father. "For the whole family. Your poor mother is rolling in her grave."

They began to follow Sokolovitch and Liz. The brothers took
turns reading the local paper in a pizza parlor across the street from
the French bakery-café. Several days were wasted, but finally, on a
Friday, they saw the teacher and the student together. Toward the
end of the third week, the brothers had become convinced Liz was
involved with the old professor. No longer able to hide their disgust, the brothers stopped talking to her. They ate silently or sat
at the table grinding their teeth. Consumed by her friendship with
Sokolovitch and used to the natural rift between her and her family,
Liz paid no attention. . . .

Still feeling the fingers of Sokolovitch's insane son on her arms
and neck, Liz went into the kitchen and poured herself some lemonade in a tall glass. She sat at the kitchen table and stared at blooming
geraniums on the windowsill. The old refugee heated up her dinner:
spaghetti with thick meat sauce. Liz was home earlier than usual.
Her father leaned back in a boxy chair, examining his blackish nails.
Her brothers gave her malicious looks, which she gladly ignored. A
sports commentator yelled something from the TV screen.

BOTH OF SOKOLOVITCH'S HANDS rested on the cane's carved
handle. The sand was wet; it had rained a lot during the first week

of May. A spindle consisting of wood chips, plastic wreckage, straw, claws, and pieces of broken shells stretched in both directions, separating the dunes and the greenish line of the surf.

"Liz, I must tell you something very serious."

"Didn't you promise?" she said, squinting. "Please, Felix, please don't be so grim. Look at the beautiful sky, at these full-bodied clouds. Light comes out of them heavy and damp. Like blue milk."

Brakes squeaked somewhere nearby. Sokolovitch turned his head to look at the parking lot. Still alone in the lot, his Buick sparkled through the gaps between the beach plum bushes.

"Felix, is that a seagull or a cormorant? Over there, at the top of the dune. Farther to your right, there, right there."

"I can't see it."

Tiptoeing, Liz put her left arm around his neck. Her right arm gently turned his head in the direction of the dunes.

"Perhaps we should be going, my dear."

Sokolovitch stepped back and separated himself from his student's arms. He looked at her silently. Then he spoke.

"If I could only see you every day. That's all I need. Just for a few minutes." Liz pressed her finger to his melting lips. "Just to walk on the beach with you every now and then. But, Liz, you know yourself that's im—"

Brakes again squealed somewhere close, behind the dunes. A runaway sun tore through the barrier of clouds. Straight at them, alongside the spindle of ocean debris, a truck was speeding. "Linore and Sons. World's Crunchiest Pickles. Retail and Wholesale." The truck turned around and stopped in their path. Liz's father and two brothers jumped out of the cab.

"Liz, they're hoodlums. Run! Don't let them get you! Scream!"

Short, grizzly, and muscular, the three men looked alike. They ran up to Sokolovitch and Liz and then split up. The father went after Liz, grabbed her across the waist and hips, and carried her to the truck. The brothers jumped on the old professor.

The brothers kicked him in the stomach and the flanks where the kidneys are. Sokolovitch lost his gold-rimmed glasses in the fighting. "Scum," Sokolovitch wheezed out. "Scream, Liz, scream!" He turned his head to where the truck had stopped before the attack, but it was no longer there—only a russet maze of rushes met the professor's eye. One syllable, *Liz-Liz-Liz*, pulsated through his brain. After the brothers knocked him to the ground, they pounded him on the head with their fists, taking turns. Liz screamed from the truck, clamped to the vinyl seat by her father's hands. Lying on his back and trying to evade the blows, Sokolovitch briefly passed out. The brothers held him down, pressing on his arms with their knees.

Overcoming a fiery pain in his back, Sokolovitch shook the brothers off and raised himself to his knees. Measuring with a shrug just how much strength was still left in his big arms and shoulders, he grabbed each brother by the neck and knocked their temples together, making the sound of falling bricks. Sokolovitch pressed their heads into the sand, his whole great body vibrating with whatever powers and desires it had remaining, and kept up the pressure until blood started flowing from their ears and nostrils, until they began to quiver under his hands like two small frogs pinned to a dissecting board. . . .

Sokolovitch then got up and walked in the direction of the blurry boundary between sky and sea. Feeling dizzy and weak in his legs, he collapsed in the water. Liz fluttered before his eyes, her tender smile, a closeup of her turquoise earrings, their table at La Baguetterie, her disappearing steps on a wet campus alley, finally a sweet fog of memories. He was dressing hastily: starched shirt, cuff links, suspenders, handkerchief. He was definitely going to be late to class. He cut himself twice while shaving in the Parisian apartment on rue des Marroniers. Looking out the window and dabbing his father's stiff cologne on cheeks and chin, Felix Sokolovitch worried that his voice would tremble again when he said "hello" to Lise Vernakoff on the way to the Lycée.

A Sunday Walk to the Arboretum

THROUGH THE EMACIATED DUSK of February's last weekend, Danny Kantor sailed the sea of suburbia. He approached his destination, a crimeless colonial town. Esther had been living here for almost five years now, getting a doctorate in Soviet history at one of the country's oldest universities and pretending that she didn't have to deal with the idiots and scoundrels of the real world. And Danny—Danny liked to believe that with the exception of geniuses, who wake up in the middle of the night to jot down a formula on the wallpaper of their vatic dreams, graduate students were merely delaying their crushing descent to reality. He had left graduate school after passing his qualifiers. It had been almost seven years, and he had rarely regretted his decision not to become an academic.

Danny tried to concentrate on Monday's business meeting with a Swedish partner, but his mind traveled to that miniature campus in the Berkshires where he had taught at the summer language institute for the last time in his life. Teaching was like feeding one's own liver to greedy, ungrateful eaglets. The stuffy night in the middle of June when he and Esther had first loved each other, ferns bloomed in the darkness, and weightless spiderwebs came between their faces. She was not in his class, and they hadn't spoken much before that night. When he met Esther for a drink, she was wearing a sleeveless blue cotton dress and clogs, worn by few American young women at the time. She had a skimpy haircut that made her nose look refined. Her legs were a little bit short, but her long dress concealed it. She had dimples when she smiled, and her eyes shone with a mixture of desire and death that Danny associated with lovemaking. They left their ales half full on the tavernous table and walked hand in hand to an abandoned quarry on the edge of a pine forest. There, on a huge cold boulder, they made love, and Danny saw a giant firebug light the forest for one second, and then the world came back to him in the form of Esther's trifoleum pressed against his temple, her fingers groping about his nape, her pupils pushing out of the irises. Later, lying in each other's arms on the mossy boulder, they made their first confessions to each other.

Esther's father had died of a heart attack when she was seven. Her mother never remarried, and Esther herself linked procreation with a fear of dying. Danny had a different view of the matter that he had inherited from his Litvak great-grandfather, who was murdered in August 1941 outside Kovno. His great-grandfather had written in one of his labyrinthine treatises that love awarded a foretaste of the world to come, which meant to Danny that when making love, we die but for a moment and enter another dimension. . . .

Danny's silver Audi traversed the main college artery with its upscale clothing stores, record shop, cozy bookstore café, and bars and restaurants. He had been here before, but never on a Saturday and not since abandoning his graduate studies and joining his uncle and cousins in the Scandinavian furniture business his mother's father had started in the late 1950s. Back in graduate school, Danny used to come down here from Manhattan at least every other month to work with the papers of the Yiddish poet Shlomo Slivka. Slivka had died in exile, in Kazakhstan, soon after the war, but his niece had managed to preserve most of his archive. Later she emigrated from Poland and sold the archive to this university's library. Slivka wrote exuberant sonnets about Jewish bird-catchers and fishmongers, about jealous innkeepers and their young—and almost chaste—wives. He sang about other things long gone, destroyed, and forgotten, like the Jewish market towns of Galicia and Volhynia.

A blue-ink printout with Esther's directions pointed Danny to a purple Gambrel with white trim. He ended up driving past it, twice, until he finally noticed a bright-red scooter. The scooter— Esther's—was chained to the black railings of the side porch. A bottle of wine like a grenade under his arm, Danny walked to the unlit front entrance. He knocked fiercely, but no one answered. Vintage Esther Levinsson, Danny thought as he contemplated having a drink in the town center and coming back later. The door squeaked, and a wrinkled bulldog stuck out his muzzle and barked.

"It's okay, Balthazar, he's a friend," said Esther's voice.

Esther opened the door and stepped back into the semidarkness of a musty stairwell. She had longer hair and tortoise-shell glasses now. In her black skirt, gray shirt, and black wool cardigan she looked older, like a thirty-something Italian or Spanish intellectual—a journalist or a high school teacher or perhaps an anarchist.

They hugged, unsurely, and Esther led him upstairs.

"When did you start wearing glasses?" Danny asked.

As he climbed the stairs, he shamelessly looked under Esther's skirt, seeing the white strips of her nakedness between her black underwear and gray wool thigh-highs. She used to wear men's underpants as a form of protest, Danny recalled.

After the first flight of stairs, Esther opened a peeling door and then shut it after the bulldog hurried in.

"He's my housemate's. Such a pain."

"The dog or the housemate?"

"The dog, stupid," and Esther's "stupid" sounded tender and inviting.

Esther's thick black hair now showed streaks of grayish yellow.

"Soon after you left California," she said and gave him a sad smile. Danny looked through a round stairwell window and remembered San Francisco Bay at dusk when he had first seen it from the airplane. Bridges fallen on their knees. Mosaics of lights on leaden water.

At the time Esther had been getting her master's at Stanford. Danny had come to visit, his first time in California. The papers were swollen with Anita Hill and Judge Thomas. Driving to a friend's house in San Anselmo the following day, they could see the work of the Oakland fire: smoldering luxury hotels, chalky clouds, stray antelopes from the municipal zoo running aimlessly across the burned slopes of the freeway and the golf courses. The midday air was heady with the ether of burning eucalyptus trees. Only when they got to San Anselmo did they feel the nearness of the Marin County beaches, the salt and iodine of the ocean air. They both knew they were breaking up, and yet they both wanted to reenact the summer when they had been together. Esther's friends had a condo off the main street, around the corner from a Russian restaurant, Troika. They dropped off their things and went to a hot-tub garden. In the tub with its aromatic steam and New Age music they made love under the clear autumnal stars of the Pacific.

"My favorite view," with her right hand Esther pointed to the round stairwell window. Outside, the darkness was starless, distended. "Did I tell you my sisters were coming for dinner?"

"All four of them?"

"Ha ha. No, just Paula and Wendy with the kids. Oh, and Rick, Paula's beau. He's going to the concert with us."

Danny had met all of Esther's four sisters only once, at a barbecue at her mother's house in White Plains. An Ashkenazi parade, Danny remembered thinking at the time. Now, as he greeted two of the Levinsson sisters, he couldn't help reflecting that in a few years Esther's hair would be as mercilessly gray as Wendy's, that her cheeks would acquire the carmine blush Paula had, never mind the noses, hips, and breasts.

Esther's apartment was too small to hold a dinner party. There was no table or chairs in the living room that doubled as her bedroom, only a futon without a frame and a lamp without a lampshade. The other room, the "study," had unfinished boards and a black door resting on cinder blocks. Esther's bookshelves and desk, the ascetic furnishings of the eternal student.

They ate downstairs in the housemate's quarters. The owner of the obese bulldog named after one of the Magi was a violinist who made a living by private lessons. He was short and rotund, with long, thin hair. His lower lip shoveled the air. Danny followed the flight of the violinist's hands as he showed Esther where to find dishes and place mats. Dressed in mustard cords and a purple sweatshirt, the violinist led his next victim, a gloomy Asian boy of seven or eight, upstairs to Esther's place. The boy's father, a tall Teutonic gentleman of about fifty, followed them. He wore a navy blazer and didn't say hello to Esther's guests.

Spicy seaweed salad was one of the appetizers, and with it the dinner guests drank Danny's Barolo. After the appetizers came dark brown broth with buckwheat noodles. Esther had gotten more fanciful about vegetarianism, having now excluded everything that had ever breathed or come from a breathing creature, including milk and yogurt. The main course consisted of Chinese steamed dumplings with cabbage filling. They dipped them in soy sauce and chewed slowly and rhythmically. Rick, Paula's beau, who wasn't Jewish, played with Wendy's two kids. He picked up a dumpling and carved out a mouth and a pair of eyes. The pasty face came out too repulsive to amuse the children.

"Time to schlep," said Esther, after which they all got up and carried the dishes into the kitchen. Danny volunteered to climb upstairs to get everybody's coats. The myopic wunderkind and his teacher were playing a duet.

SERENA ORTEGA'S CONCERT at the university theater was the official reason for his visit. The reason or the pretext—Danny hadn't quite decided. Wendy, the third sister, couldn't stay for the concert because of her kids. On the balcony, sitting a few rows apart from Esther's sister Paula and her Rick, Esther and Danny were relatively alone for the first time since California. For two full years they had been out of touch. He didn't even know she had moved back East. Danny had preserved and occasionally reread the gorgeous letters Esther had sent him from Stanford: a thick batch of interior monologues describing pockmarked, balding executives on the train, the smells and colors of autumn in the Bay Area, her dreams. One of them, Danny still remembered, involved Lenin and his wife, Nadezhda K. Krupskaya, and another was about Esther and Danny sharing a park bench with an old black lady with violets on her straw hat. Even though he could never read through Esther's rambling letters, his photographic memory had stored some passages: "I don't think today really existed. It started late but then it was five"; "another New York Jew, from Long Island, sort of misanthropic, messed up in a nice way"; "I have been thinking about Khrushchev. I never really cared about him until I started to understand the rage of a deposed monarch."

Esther touched his hand—a wet leaf falling on a park bench.

"Do you remember Maine?" whispered Esther.

Danny was playing a mind game. He wasn't going to let Esther rummage through their shared past. Did he remember Maine? They had gone up there in August, after the Berkshire summer program had ended and before Esther returned to California. They had driven along the coast, stopping for the night in cheap motels with curious names: Jimmo's, De Loin's, Lobster Trap. They had had the same glorious routine every day of the week: driving in the morning, then the beach, dinner and drinks in some local saloon, after which they went back to their room. They both had liked the idea of a routine with lovemaking at the end of the day. They wanted to believe their long life together would be like that Maine vacation, with shiny pebbles on the beach, solicitous bartenders, and days unfolding in anticipation of love. It was a week of celebrations, a new life: Danny was quitting graduate school; Esther would finish her master's and be with him.

Nodding to familiar songs, Danny tried to think of the day he first wanted to break it off with Esther. It was sometime at the beginning of October, a record warm October in New England. He had woken up one day feeling that Esther no longer occupied the space and time of his life, that he couldn't shut his eyes and imagine her, that he didn't know her anymore. That's when he had gone to visit her in the Bay Area. After the farewell time in San Anselmo, he had left California hoping that Esther had released him. At first he tried playing at friendship, but Esther returned his notes unopened. The family furniture business in Framingham, Massachusetts, which Danny had joined, was keeping him preoccupied. He stopped writing poetry. For a while he was seeing Alessandra Celli, a madly jealous Italian economist from Perugia, with whom he had started a fling soon after moving to Boston, even while Esther was still in the picture. Then he had met a woman from the Brazilian consulate; then came Mercedes the art dealer, then a redhead nurse from St. Elizabeth's, then a Boston Brahmin lawyer, and, finally, a Danish designer living in a church converted into condos. He was beginning to think he had been vaccinated against Jewish women. . . .

"She's amazing!" Esther said to Paula and Rick, who were waiting outside the theater.

"Should we all go somewhere for a drink?" Danny suggested. He wasn't sure he wanted to be alone with Esther.

They ended up having tea at Esther's place. They all sat on the floor in Esther's bedroom and ate the nondairy carrot cake Paula and Rick had brought. There wasn't much conversation—mostly scraps of gossip about Esther's extraordinarily large *meshpocha*. Paula, like Esther's other sisters, was residually resentful of Danny. Seated against the wall, Danny sipped his green tea. His heart was weary.

"Do you want to go to bed?" Esther asked him as Rick's white Jeep was backing out of the driveway.

"Sure."

"You can have my bedroom if you want."

"What about you?"

"I'll sleep downstairs. There's a fold-out sofa."

"Won't Balthazar bother you?" Danny tried to joke it off.

"No, I'll be fine," Esther sounded perturbed. "Do you still like oatmeal for breakfast?"

"Absolutely."

"Good night, Danny boy—are you still 'Danny boy'?"

"Sleep tight, Esther. See you in the A.M."

In Esther's bedroom with its slanted ceilings, bare walls, and two windows without curtains Danny lay in bed and listened to the swooshing outside. He couldn't sleep, feeling a mixture of guilt and disappointment. The insomniac's midnight rotgut. Talking to Esther on the phone the past several months, he had begun to reexperience that giddy sensation he had had when they first met, during the summer of their love. Then came Esther's invitation to come down for dinner and the concert. And now here he was, lying awake, alone in Esther's chilly bed.

There was a timid tapping at the door, a child's or an old lady's, and Esther came in. She was wearing flannel plaid pajamas, slippers, and glasses. For some reason (and it wasn't just the name coincidence), she reminded Danny of a girl he had grown up with in Brookline, Esther Hulot, whose father was a blind accordionist.

"Hi," Esther said. "I couldn't sleep. I thought maybe you would still be up. Are you cold?"

"A little bit," Danny replied. Then he asked, "Is there another blanket?"

"Should be one in the closet."

The bulldog suddenly burst into the room and attacked Danny's comforter.

"Balthazar, get out of here, nasty dog!"

Esther chased the dog out and shut the door.

LIKE A JAILBIRD on a Sunday morning, Danny woke up strangely serene. He had the whole day instantly mapped out in his head. The experiment at rekindling the past would be over with, and he would go back to Boston, away from Esther's expectant eyes.

He pulled on jeans and headed for the bathroom. He saw Esther sitting at the desk in her study and sipping coffee from a red mug.

"How about if I take you out for Sunday brunch? Is that diner on Main Street still open?"

"You mean the Lebanese place?"

"Yeah, what's it called, the . . . the Cedar House?"

"I don't usually go there. Too greasy."

Esther's sulkiness made him want to flirt with her.

They sat for a while on the floor in Esther's study, she in a bathrobe and Danny in jeans and the T-shirt he had slept in. They sipped pumpkin-flavored coffee. Always Halloween here, a moveable Halloween?

"So how are your parents?" Esther asked.

"They're doing well," Danny gratefully replied. "Mom still teaches part-time at Tufts, dad's practicing. Many of his patients are Russian. Russian Jews who still believe in the power of a doctor from Moscow."

"That's funny," was all Esther said.

"Yes, pretty funny. My dad has been here thirty years, and they still think of him as a Russian doctor."

Danny got up to run a morning bath; there was no shower in Esther's bathroom. The tub stood on rusty lion's paws.

Washing himself, Danny heard the muffled sounds of two violins reaching up from below. The housemate was already giving his first lesson. Danny was glad he didn't have to torment students. He shaved, threw the toiletries in his weekend bag, pulled his coat on, and trotted down the stairs. Outside he saw Esther sitting in a lawn chair by the front door. She was wearing a pair of faded black jeans, a coarse maroon sweater, and a lettuce green scarf. They drove in Danny's car to the center of town and parked across the street from the Cedar House.

He ordered pancakes and tea with lemon. Esther asked for a bagel with nothing on it, and a cup of herbal tea. They didn't say much during brunch.

"What do you want to do now, Danny boy?" Esther asked when they came out of the diner.

"Let's go for a walk in the arboretum. I used to take breaks from working at the library and go there to look at different trees."

"I've never been to the arboretum, isn't that bizarre? All these years."

"I'll show you my favorite oak tree," Danny said.

They walked for about ten minutes. They entered through the arboretum's wrought-iron gates with gilded laurel wreaths, then took the main alley. From afar, the trunks of tulip trees looked like frog skin. On their way, they spotted white crocuses on a sunny clearing. Early this year.

"Look, look," Esther tugged at his sleeve. "That's Homunculus."

A little man with a hunched back was approaching from the opposite direction on a bicycle from the turn of the century, with an enormous leading wheel and a tiny back one. The span of the front wheel made the tiny rider look even smaller. He stopped a few feet from where Esther and Danny were standing and jumped off to the ground. Esther introduced them. The man Esther called "Homunculus" turned out to be one of the world's leading authorities on Yiddish poetry, and Danny knew his work from his own days in graduate school. Homunculus was preparing a bilingual edition of Shlomo Slivka's works while on a fellowship at the Center for Advanced Study. He was at least a whole head shorter than Esther. He had long red hair and a thin long nose. His lips were chapped from riding in the wind. He wore a striped shirt, a bow tie, a three-piece suit, sneakers, a black beret, and a cape. He spoke English with a formidable Russian accent, having particular trouble with the *r*'s and *th*'s.

"I remember your article from 1991," Homunculus said to Danny. "Very good work. It is quite unfortunate you have—"

"That's kind of you," Danny stopped him short. "But I'm in a different line of work now," he said, remembering the time in his life when he had wanted to know everything about Slivka: every woman the poet had ever known; his favorite aphorisms; what cigarettes he smoked and whether he liked jazz. Danny had loved the research part. It was the academic scrabbling that he wasn't fit for.

"How's your work on the edition coming along?" he asked Homunculus, more or less out of politeness.

"I am the happiest person alive," said Homunculus. His eyes switched back and forth from Esther to Danny, while his smile got bigger and bigger, showing baby white teeth. "I have held Shlomo's poems in my hands. You know his fabulous sonnets, right? That was worth living for! But I must be on my way. I owe it to dear Shlomo's memory. Good-bye, Esther. Farewell, Mr. Kantor."

Like a grasshopper, Homunculus hopped in the saddle and rode off. His cape caught a gust of wind.

"He's so ridiculous," Esther lifted her left brow.

"I thought he was kind of charming," Danny said.

"Shlomo Slivka is all he can talk about."

"He seems like a nice guy."

"A bore, that's what he is," Esther sliced.

"But you went out with him, didn't you?" Danny asked and immediately regretted asking.

"Who told you?"

"Just heard it through the grapevine."

"I thought you were through with the grapevine."

"Well, I guess not quite through," Danny smiled and looked away. "Come on, Esther, it's nothing to be ashamed of," he added. "He's a brilliant scholar."

"He's not you," said Esther.

They walked silently for a while and then turned off the main alley.

"This black oak I'm taking you to, it's so mighty that I used to think that, it has a male soul living in one of its hollows instead of a dryad's." Danny tried to concoct a mythological joke.

"So you think the bigger trees are male?" For the first time, Esther sounded confrontational.

"I don't want to argue body politics. That I'm definitely through with. I just want to show you a beautiful tree."

Danny looked around for his black oak but couldn't find it anywhere.

"So-o-o-o, where's your famous mighty oak, Danny boy?" Esther drew out the question.

"I don't know what the heck is going on. I must've forgotten my way around. It's been a few years . . . "

They walked for another hundred yards and saw a huge stump and mounds of fresh amber sawdust.

"They cut it down!" Danny screamed. "This black oak was the oldest tree in the whole arboretum. I don't get it."

Esther squatted before the stumps and tried counting the year rings on its shear. Finally, she got bored and gave up.

"You want to go?" Esther brightened up, looking almost cheerful.

"Sure," Danny replied.

They walked back to Main Street, where his silver Audi was parked.

"Would you like me to take you home?" he asked Esther.

"No, I think I'll go to the library for a couple of hours. Bye." She gave Danny a quick hug and whispered "drive careful" in his ear. He watched her cross the street and head toward the main gate of the campus. Like a squirrel, Esther's little satchel jumped on her back.

Danny smoked a cigarette, then got into the car, took out an apple from his suede weekend bag, moved the bag to the backseat, and drove off. He was relieved to be leaving this innocuous university town, where all parents dreamed of their sons' or daughters' getting an education. He wouldn't be returning here for a while. Other people will study Shlomo Slivka's ardent sonnets at the rare book and manuscript library, Danny thought. Other people will walk in the arboretum under the old oaks and sycamores. And other people will love Esther.

The interstate had already offered its sacrificial raccoons to the late Sunday morning traffic. Danny lowered the window, and wet chilly air carried the taste of dormant earth to his lips and nostrils. He reached into his jacket pocket for a handkerchief and felt a little envelope next to a box of Tic Tacs. He took out the envelope and read the words "Danny boy" ebbing away across it.

Horse Country

THEY MET BY THE DEPARTURE BOARD. It was late April, but the spring was heavy, wearisome, with cold nights and mornings, frequent rains, and swollen, still unopened buds. The midday station was empty and quiet because westbound trains either had arrived or were running late. They still had half an hour before their train for Charlesville departed. They stood on the platform, leaning on a gray and dark blue lantern post with coiled castings. Posts like that have almost disappeared, except at the very old train stations.

Pete Krichevsky was taking Lexie to Russian Meadow to ride horses. She wore a long skirt that swept the ground, suede boots, and a short brown coat. Like a page, Pete carried her black gloves because she didn't like to wear them and removed and lost them at every possible occasion. He stood with his back to the track, embracing Lexie and snuggling up to her with all his weight, chest to chest, his eyelashes sometimes tickling her cheek. She said she liked his long eyelashes. Once, she had even measured them with a thread and then threatened to apply mascara in his sleep.

Pete heard the train coming in. Only then, as the halting cars brought the warm taste of burning coal under his tongue, did he finally believe that they were going away together. Before everything, when they had spoken for the first time at the racetrack, Lexie had told him about her golden dream of riding "real" horses "in the wild." And now, bending to pick up Lexie's weekend bag with the whip jutting out of it, he looked at her, and he saw how she was flushed with impatience, how her breathing quickened. She was the first to jump on the train and run toward a vacant compartment with two dank, fern green bunks. The long-armed conductor swore at her, something about "little city bitches," and Pete had to admonish him for his inexplicable malice.

"Do you remember the centaurs?" he asked Lexie as the train was pulling off.

"Centaurs?"

"As in Greek mythology."

"No, why?"

"I don't know. For some reason centaurs have been on my mind the entire morning."

"And . . . ?"

He put her hand between both of his.

"One of the myths goes like this. The Greeks invited the centaurs to a feast. The centaurs had heard about the abundance of viands at Greek feasts and decided to attend. There was much wine at the feast, but the Greeks mixed it with cold water and didn't get drunk. The centaurs drank a lot of undiluted wine and fell to the ground, intoxicated and powerless. The Greeks attacked their women and ravished them."

"God, you're too learned for me." Lexie paused for a minute, biting a nail with chipped polish. "I haven't read any of that stuff. But I have read a lot about real horses. Articles about horses, novels about horses, poems about horses—"

"Memoirs of horses . . . ," he inserted.

The train had already left the city behind and was making its way northwest. The door was half open, and anyone walking through the car could peep inside their compartment, where Pete was now lying on the lower bunk, his head in Lexie's lap. Outside the window, summer cottages bobbed up and down.

"Did you make it all up?" Lexie asked. "About the horse farm, Uncle Vic? And everything else, too?"

"What makes you think so?"

"Because I think you just wanted to take me away from the city, where my darling parents are always bugging me, where everybody e-mails and calls, and you can't have me all to yourself?"

He didn't say anything, kissing the knuckles of Lexie's cold hands.

About halfway there, an old man with military decorations on his double-breasted jacket occupied the opposite bunk in their compartment. One still occasionally runs across old men like that on trains. The man dozed off, and Lexie and Pete didn't speak the remaining four hours. Pete looked out the window, trying to follow the flashing landscape. All the while his eyes searched for horses. And only once, when they passed a long water meadow girdled by a river, did he see a horse and rider. They probably wanted to cross the tracks and so stood waiting.

"Look, Pete, look—a centaur."

"Hey, I wonder if he can see you in the moving train? Why don't you wave to him?"

The train finally rested against the siding, shaking fumes away in a long convulsion. The Charlesville platform was desolate. They drank coffee in a cafeteria under the low vault of the station. Lexie had brought chicken sandwiches from home. The grease, now congealed, tasted salty and lemony. At the cafeteria Lexie also bought a danish with apple jam. She didn't eat it, only nibbled the crust.

A local train for Russian Meadow, a town ten miles east of Uncle Vic's horse farm, was not calling until daybreak, so they sat on a cold wooden bench in the waiting area.

"And what if the train doesn't come?" asked Lexie.

"Then we'll take a taxi. Sleep now. You'll see everything soon."

"Horses?"

"Hearses!"

"You're a goofball, Pete."

She slept on his shoulder, resting her hand on his jacket pocket. Pete was nervous. He was afraid of missing the connecting train. He worried about the night hunters out for his wallet. Then the train came. Lexie slept for an hour in the empty car. She didn't see the sunrise.

ON THE PLATFORM in Russian Meadow Lexie immediately spotted an old woman selling sunflower seeds, bought some, and began to crack them. The train pulled away, stealing images of Lexie printed on the timeworn windows.

The derelict bus—not really a bus, but a charabanc—went along the main street of the village, stopping often to drop off exhausted-looking women with heavy grocery bags. Snow seemed to have melted a week earlier, and the dried-up streets were already choked with dust. The driver took them almost to the entrance of the sanatorium at the end of the village. The horse farm's iron gates were behind them to the left. At the foot of a pine forest the long village street ended abruptly. The bus turned around on yellow sand and headed back to Russian Meadow, beating powdery clouds out of the road.

Lexie gave Pete her coat to carry, keeping on her old black sweater, washed many times and shrunk, so that in it her breasts were lifted and shaped as in a charcoal portrait. They walked along a path, stepping over hoof prints and trampling last year's faded pine needles into the ground.

"Remember I told you about the consumptives?"

"Sort of vaguely," Lexie said, screwing up her left eye.

"They live right behind those gates. A whole community of TB patients. They take walks around the forest and sometimes in the meadows that belong to the horse farm. They are silent, sad-looking folk at the sanatorium."

"So how do they treat the poor patients?"

"Well, that's the funny part—with fresh air and rest, for the most part. Plus, every morning they get two huge jars of mare's milk, brought in on a cart. They used to think that fermented mare's milk has medicinal power for TB patients. But now—"

"Mare's milk? Is this a holistic clinic or something?" Lexie asked.

"You could say that. And who do you think tends the herd of milch mares with colts?"

"I guess that would be your friend Uncle Vic."

The path brushed against a wide wicket gate, repaired many times in many places. A wooden fence of a man's height, bound on top with coils of barbed wire, stretched away from both sides of the gate, flanked by an island of gray and slate blue grassland. The fence dropped down the slope of a dark ravine.

"Uncle Vic! You've got company!"

Old paint rained from the door onto the stoop as Pete knocked. While the insides of the house stirred, while bare feet shuffled to the door, Lexie settled on one of the saddles that was left on the ground near the stoop. She began to unweave the entangled stirrups of another one, a Cossack saddle with faded embroidery on the sides.

Uncle Vic came out onto the stoop, tightening his jacket closer to his naked hairless chest.

"Hello there, so you came after all."

"It's good to see you, Uncle Vic."

"I thought about you this winter. Especially when I saddled Baby. I'd be thinking: Such a great guy, stayed here with me—and not even a postcard? But here you are, sir, please come in. What are we doing standing in the doorway?"

Lexie raised her eyes and came toward them.

"Pete has told me so much about you," she said to Uncle Vic. "My name is Alexandra, but Pete calls me 'Lexie.'"

"Alexandra, that's a Russian name," said Uncle Vic.

"Yes, my parents are from Russia, but I was born here."

"Honored to meet you, Miss Alexandra," said Uncle Vic and offered Lexie his pine-bark hand for a shake.

"Thank you for letting us stay, Uncle Vic."

"I'm glad you folks came out here. I don't get a lot of visitors."

"Uncle Vic," Lexie gave the old herdsman a smile, "do you think I could wash up and change? We've been traveling since yesterday afternoon."

"Sure, sure," said Uncle Vic and led the guests inside the house. "There's a wash basin in your room."

Lexie went into the room. Uncle Vic and Pete stayed in the large, dimly lit kitchen with high-pitched floors and an earthy smell of old potatoes. Pete put two bottles of vodka and half-a-dozen tins on the table.

"That's our contribution, Uncle Vic. So tell me, how's the year been?"

"What can I say, we survive. Sometimes Randy drops by. Do you remember him, the one with a crooked nose?"

"I do," answered Pete.

"Well, he stops by. But mostly I'm here by myself. Remember the skewbald stallion, the one who was still unbroken the last time you were here?"

"I do."

"Last week there were races in town, and I rode him. And we came in first! Skewbald, he is a God-blessed stallion."

"Uncle Vic, is it all right if Lexie rides him?" Pete asked. "She doesn't like fillies."

"Why not? He's calm now. Are you going to be here a while?"

"Three or four days. We'll see how it goes. We'll see about the weather."

THE DOOR from the guest room to the kitchen was half open. Lexie stood near the washstand, stripped to the waist, her head tossed back. Lapping up handfuls of water, she was washing her neck, shoulders, breasts, and underarms.

"Pete, get out. Now!"

"I want to watch your cleansing ritual," Pete said with his serious-unserious intonation.

Light from the window cast half-shadows on Lexie while leaving Pete in the darkness. He took a towel from the back of a cast-iron chair and unfolded it as he came up to her from behind. He wrapped Lexie up so that under each of his rounded palms a breast was found. He pulled her up to him and began to kiss her neck and shoulders, licking off drops of faintly salty water.

"Crazy man, you think only of sex."

"Tss, he can hear everything."

"Good for him. All right, Pete," Lexie tore herself from his hands. "Didn't we come here to ride horses? So put on your boots and let's go."

On the stoop, Uncle Vic sat smoking a thick stogie. The sweet shag smoke crawled under his cap and into his orange hair, sweaty from the sun.

"Uncle Vic, my good man, is it okay if we go riding now?"

"Can you manage the saddling? I don't feel like going over to the stable right now."

"And where is Skewbald?"

"Remember Baby? He's two stalls from her."

"To the left?"

"Yes. I mean, to the right. If you run into problems, come get me. And don't ride Baby too hard, she's still a young filly."

They walked to the long green stable. Its urgent smell hit their nostrils. Wisps of hay came flying from under their boots, and their steps echoed on the dark stone floor. It's difficult to run on a stable floor, and their feet couldn't move very fast.

Baby, as if remembering Pete, was as friendly as she had been in the summer when he had last seen her. He put the bridle on her and led her to the big barrel filled with black water. She gulped thirstily and didn't want to stop.

Uncle Vic hated saddle blankets, considering them a racetrack invention. He was a real herdsmen, one of the last few. Pete had to saddle up right on Baby's sleek, clean red back. While he was watering and then saddling Baby, Lexie saddled Skewbald. From the corner of his eye, sneaking a glance under his hand, he saw how Skewbald at first refused to suck in his belly, not letting Lexie tighten the saddle girth. But Lexie rubbed herself against his neck, below his ear, then slapped his flank, and away went his bloated belly.

They took the horses outside the stable, mounted, and rode diagonally along the yard to the gate. It was only the end of April, and the fields hadn't yet begun to blossom. But the thyme bushes, having spent all winter under snow, had already straightened up. Water from melted snow had chewed and tramped down the speary leaves of last year's feather grass. Yellow foalfoots and hazy-blue cornflowers shot out here and there from the waxen gray-and-purple carpet. Fierce thistle stems, dark crimson and brown, jutted out of the earth. Unearthly sounds squelched up from the bottom of the ravine they passed and left behind. The sounds of the wild fields are usually replete with whistling and singing, rustling and sighing. Calling and echoing sounds. Cooling and soothing to the ear. As they climbed along the slope of the ravine, Pete felt that there, ahead, the fields smelled of honey and savory—of oblivion—and he urged Baby on.

"Hey, Lexie, do you want to gallop?" he asked, without thinking.

"Ah-Ah-Ah-ahhahahah. Peeeeeete."

"Lexie, the fields are endless—ahahahah!"

"Yes! They're endless. Spring's endless. So long, Uncle Vic! So long milch mares with foals! We're never coming back . . . "

Lexie was galloping just ahead. Her body was bent forward, following the arch of Skewbald's neck, pressing tightly against him. In a few minutes Baby's neck turned hot and sweaty, as the filly's breathing grew heavier.

"Let's take a break," Pete shouted. "I can't ride her so hard. Wait!"

"I can't stop him . . . "

She disappeared behind a silhouette of thistles.

Pete dismounted and let Baby go. She took a few steps and stopped, looking for something in the grass.

"Well, Baby, little girl, what're you doing?" he said to the filly, stroking her neck. "What're you looking for? That's a good girl."

He lay down on his stomach. Ants crawled along his sleeves, falling into last year's insect holes and between stems of feather grass. He pressed his ear to the ground and listened. No hooves could be heard. Birds chirped somewhere beyond the edge of the fields. He closed his eyes.

"Pete," Lexie yelled when she rode up to him from behind.

Pete sat up, turned his head and saw that the top buttons of her French blue flannel shirt were undone.

"Pete, I love you so much for bringing me here. This is ecstasy."

"Glad you're having fun," he said, feeling the throbs of longing.

"It was so great. Look, Pete, look. Skewbald has such big eyes. You can hardly see the pupils."

She got down from the saddle. They lay for a while in the shade on the border of a pine forest. Then the air became heavy with gnats, and they returned to the farmhouse.

LISTENING TO THE RATTLE of boiling whole potatoes, Pete opened tins: pickled herring and smoked sardines in oil. Then, tears sprouting in his eyes, he sliced a large onion into rings. When the potatoes were done, they sat down to dinner. Pete poured warm vodka into three stocky glasses.

"So Uncle Vic," he said after they had had a couple of drinks. "Tell how you ended up here."

"You've heard the story."

"Yeah, but Lexie hasn't."

"Not much to tell. This stud farm was built by Mr. Korshunoff, a Russian émigré. Back in the 1930s. And he brought the trotters here. You know about the trotters—they have really long shins." Uncle Vic poured himself some more vodka and drank up.

"Actually my wife dragged me out here. We used to live in Victory, you know, up north, near the border. They breed a lot of horses up in Victory. Real nice horses. Beautiful coats, especially the reds! I liked it up there, even the winters. So my wife, she heard that they needed men to work with horses down here in Russian Meadow. They offered free housing, and that was it for my wife. So we moved. And after we came, she hated it here. She said she was bored. During the first winter, things went from bad to worse. She couldn't milk the mares, and that was part of the job: the farm has a deal with the TB place next door. When spring came, she packed up and left. To her mother's, so she said. And I haven't heard from her since. But that's all right, we never lived well together anyway. So horses was all I had left. Natalie, a widow from the village, now comes to milk the mares in the morning. She sometimes helps around the house. I wouldn't milk them myself. It's a nasty business to milk horses and cut their tails to make cello bows."

They drank, ate and talked some more. Then they ran out of conversation topics and sat without speaking. With her fork Lexie drove a cold potato from one side of the plate to the other.

"Thanks for dinner," she finally said. "I think I'll go to bed now. See you in the morning."

"Have a good sleep," said Uncle Vic. "By the way," he added, "the bed is some sort of an antique. Came with the place. The guy before me found it in the old farmhouse when they were taking it down. He told me the Russian gentleman used to sleep in this bed with his wife when she came out here from the city to visit. She liked to ride the trotters. Perhaps it's true, I don't know. But it's a good bed. I slept a whole winter on it with my wife."

Pete followed Lexie to their room. He couldn't find the switch on the wall and unscrewed the bulb out of the low ceiling. Then he came up to Lexie and embraced her. His fingers, as if by themselves, were already unbuttoning her stubborn shirt. Lexie didn't move. And didn't speak. Through the curtainless window she looked at the outline of the stables. At the dark horizon of the fields. The Archer.

When she was completely naked, he took her up to the bed, kissing the moonlit scratches on her shoulders and shoulder blades. There were strips of the moon on her hips and knees. Silvery salamanders slipped away into her lap, and his fingers chased after them. The bed was so large that they lay across it. Pete slowly kissed Lexie's neck. He kissed her ears, her feather-grass-scented locks. Again his fingers slid to her lap.

"Pete, I don't want you inside me. Just your hand. Please, not today, I don't know why. Would you please just touch me?"

"I don't get it. You know how I feel."

She sprang from underneath him.

They lay awake for a while listening to the wind whooshing through the meadows. As they were falling asleep, they heard the midnight neighing of fretting mares.

NEXT MORNING Pete went to tend the herd with Uncle Vic. He left Lexie a note. They led the groggy horses out of the stables, then drove the entire herd around a roughhewn ravine into the meadows. On the way back, Skewbald, the leader, tried to take his herd to a low-lying spot, but Uncle Vic caught up with him and pulled his tail, swearing. When Skewbald jerked away toward a field of oats, Pete chased him away from there. Not for the first time giving in to herdsmen, Skewbald galloped off toward the stables, shaking his ears.

They returned at lunchtime. Lexie, in a long, faded floral print skirt and a white linen blouse, was reading on the stoop.

"Are you hungry?" she asked. A mysterious smile teetered on her lips.

"I'm starving," Pete said. Uncle Vic nodded in agreement.

"So how's Pete doing, Uncle Vic?" Lexie asked. "Last night he told me that he wanted to become a herdsman. Begged me to stay here with him."

"Well, if that's what you want, fine. Thank God, I've got lots of room. You could milk the mares. But you'll have to get up pretty early. Stay, why not? God's country here." The herdsman sat down and rolled and lit a stogie.

For lunch they ate leftover potatoes fried with eggs and gray village bread. They finished yesterday's bottle of vodka and talked about the past. In the country, topics recur even more often than in the city. After lunch Pete felt so tired that he could barely follow the conversation. He told Lexie he was going to take a nap, kissed her, and went to their room.

He slept almost until sunset. The house was empty. Uncle Vic had probably gone off to the village; he had said something about getting new harnesses. Pete's face felt dry from sleep, but there was no water left in the washstand, and he didn't feel like going to the well. He went on foot to look for Lexie. On his way he stopped by the stable. Skewbald's stall was wide open. An empty bucket stood on the floor near the stall. In the semidarkness Pete's foot brushed against and kicked an empty bottle.

The sun was setting, moving along the elder groves at the edge of the forest. Several times along the way he turned back at the forest. He ended up wandering far into the fields. It was very quiet. The soil, not yet deeply heated and dried by the spring sun, felt damp under his feet. He occasionally bent to pick up a dry stem or a yellowed dittany leaf. It felt so good just to crush the stems and leaves between his fingers, to breathe in the bitter, cinnamony, minty scents. He climbed on top of a small hillock crowned with a pyramid of thistles that blocked his passage. He looked back. Half of the yellow globe had already dipped behind the green coniferous boundary, but it was still light out.

About a hundred yards ahead he saw Skewbald and Lexie. Flattening the thyme bushes, her clothes were scattered beside the stallion's saddle and harness. Lexie was embracing the stallion's neck and caressing his muzzle with her fingers, shoulders, cheeks, and neck. She even pulled him down so that his muzzle could reach her breasts. She was telling him something, but softly, and her voice was muffled by the distance.

Pete squatted on the hillock and watched, strangling his urge to call out her name. Lexie walked around Skewbald on tiptoes, lightly stroking his flanks and back, unweaving thistles from his tail. Then she kneeled near the stallion's front legs and clenched his left leg with both her hands, like a jug. She stroked it, then the right one, up and down, for a long time, patiently. Then she got under his belly, her hands and legs thrown around Skewbald's trunk. Then Pete saw Lexie sprawled on the stallion's back. Once again she rolled down Skewbald's back to his hind legs. It suddenly grew dark. The last thing he distinctly saw were Lexie's thin ankles, locked tightly near the stallion's waving, unbraided tail. Then all the clear spaces between woman and horse disappeared; perhaps they were closed, or perhaps filled in with darkness. Pete ran away, fearing the centaur's wrath.

He wandered around the perimeter, then finally returned to the horse farm. He lay for a while across the bed in their room, unable to think. Lexie wasn't back. Uncle Vic came in, cleared his throat, and spat into the bucket in the kitchen. A large, long-legged mosquito, of the sort falsely believed to be malarial, flew into the room and smashed itself in the corner. Pete's glance was frozen on Lexie's black sweater, on her hand mirror in the cupboard, on her makeup kit. His glance was frozen.

"Pete, you're sleeping?" Lexie woke him. "Did you have something to eat? Why not?! Why are you looking at me like that?"

Pete jumped off the bed. He put his arms around her shoulders and silently studied her for a minute.

"Lexie, my love, let's go back to the city tomorrow. Don't . . . "

He pushed her tousled locks away from her forehead, kissing her cold temples. From her ashen locks he unwove threads of horse hair and flung them to the floor.

Yom Kippur in Amsterdam

ON A LATE-SEPTEMBER AFTERNOON that looked misty from inside
the Schiphol terminal, Jake Glaz got off the Nice flight and decided
to have lunch before taking the train into Amsterdam. Although it was
only two o'clock, he was already worried about not getting enough to
eat before sunset: it was the eve of Yom Kippur. His sole reason for
stopping in Amsterdam was to avoid having to atone while in flight
over fathomless waters. Jake Glaz, who used to be called Yasha Glazman, wasn't too keen on a two-day delay in his return home to Baltimore, where he ran a division of an international travel company. But
there was nothing he could do: Yom Kippur, the Jewish Day of Atonement, was the only holiday that Jake observed "religiously."

Devouring his second sandwich with Dutch herring that tasted
nostalgically like "red fish," the cured salmon from his Soviet childhood and youth, and washing it down with Groelsch, Jake recalled
the vacation he had just spent with friends on the beach and promenade in Nice during the mornings and at the roulette tables in Monte
Carlo in the evenings. He and Erin had come up with the idea of a
September trip to the Riviera during one of their weekend visits
to Annapolis. Fluttering flags over the bay, oysters and blue crabs,
cadets in celestial uniforms, yachts striating the horizon. Attributes
of summer by the sea always made Jake yearn for a Riviera vacation
during the "velvet season," when the Mediterranean heat has sub-
sided and the French vacationers have already gone back home after
their annual August respite.

"Sweetums," Erin had said to him in her voice that was playful and yet knew no irony. "Weren't you recently reading something about Nice? A story—by Mr. Chekhov, or was it by Mr. Nabokov?"

They had been together for almost two years, and Jake loved her terminal innocence. He thought Erin was a classic American girl: German Irish, smiley and light-hearted, thin and freckle-faced, all long legs and small breasts, sneakers, jeans and big sweaters. He marveled at her capacity to live by common sense alone. He never fully understood how she could comfortably combine an in-depth knowledge of her immediate surroundings, her hometown, her fashion magazines, her government job with a languid indifference to the larger picture of the world. It's not that Erin didn't want to learn. She actually managed to memorize all the occasional bits of Jewish history that he would share with her while driving someplace or in bed after lovemaking. Yet she was always content with the small slice of life that had been served her on a green paper plate.

This trip was to have been Erin's first time on the Riviera, and Jake had wanted the trip to be an eye-opener. A travel expert that he was, he had never planned his own vacations as thoroughly as he did this time. Every day was to be a novelty for Erin: lemon groves in Menton, high society in Monte Carlo, Picasso at Cape d'Antibe and Renoir in Cagnes-sur-Mer, movies in Cannes, perfumes in Grass, fishing in Saint-Tropez. Jake had reserved a room in a quiet four-star hotel, the former residence of the Russian imperial consul, only a five-minute walk from promenade des Anglais.

By the end of April every detail of their fortnight on the Riviera had been meticulously planned; tickets and reservations had already been deposited in Jake's top desk drawer at work. And then came summer, even hotter and swampier than usually in the Baltimore area, and the closer they got to their departure date in September, the more he felt trapped in his own doubts. The whole thing all finally came together—like a simple geographic jigsaw puzzle on his computer screen—after a trip to Erin's hometown in central

Pennsylvania. Erin's uncle pestered Jake with idiotic, kindly questions about *Schindler's List.* Her elder sister referred to the yarmulkes
of Hasidic Jews she had seen in Pittsburgh as "beanies." And then
came Sunday, when he spent the morning alone in the house playing
with Nicky the dachshund while the entire family was in church.
Erin had never shoved her Catholicism down his throat; she knew
he would choke. Nor did Jake ever try to proselytize—he found the
notion intellectually offensive and very un-Jewish. Yet the personal
experiences of his friends who married non-Jews as well as the various statistics he had obtained suggested that Erin would be likely to
convert were he to ask her. He did finally ask her in the car on the
way back to Baltimore, only to discover Erin's stern loyalty to her
faith—a loyalty that he had never imagined to be so absolute. Bovine
tears glistening in her eyes, a pony tail pulled through the back of
her "Navy" baseball cap, Erin stroked his hand on the gear shift and
kept repeating again and again: "Jake, I'll give you children, I'll help
you raise them Jewish, I'll learn things, but I can't leave my faith.
Why won't you accept me?"

Jake drove on silently, shaking inwardly with anger, tossing
over in his head images of the pope greeting a Sunday crowd in the
Vatican; black and green plaid skirts on the subway in D.C.; half-a-
dozen Catholic weddings he had attended. He had previously lived
his life believing that in a Christian world a Jew ought to honor the
ways of the majority without losing his own face. And now he had
found himself so enraged with, so antagonistic toward the church,
as though it was somehow its fault that his future happiness now lay
in ruins.

"Why can't you accept me for what I am?" Erin asked him again
on the phone, a few days later.

"I do love you, Erin, but I just can't marry you. We are a small
people. The mother of my children has to be Jewish, no matter how
you slice it," Jake choked on his words. "No pun intended," he added
after a pause.

Four or five days after that, on a Saturday morning, a lanky UPS lady delivered a box for a twenty-inch television set. Inside the box Jake found all two years' worth of his presents to Erin returned in what looked like their original gift wrappings. It's some sort of a joke, he thought for an instant, unwrapping the half-full vial of the French perfume from Thanksgiving, unfolding the dark green wool wrap he had bought for her in London. His hands finally reached a thick pile at the bottom of the box. All his letters and even printed out e-mails, the faxes he liked to send her from work or sometimes from aboard the plane, and at least twenty postcards, mailed from the destinations of his regular trips—Singapore, Naples, Moscow, and São Paulo. Each mailing accurately torn in two. The whole thick pile tied with a blue silk ribbon. And a note on top: "Jake, I loved you more than anything, but not more than Jesus. One day you'll understand. Please don't try to contact me. I've changed my phone number. Bye, Er." On the floor, he sat amid presents now twice opened, gaping at the ceiling the way an insomniac gapes at his blowsy wakefulness.

Fortunately for Jake, his dearest Moscow friend, Mulya Borisov, even though a father of two girls and a paterfamilias, was still as adventurous as he was when he and Jake (still Yasha Glazman then) had their youth and studenthood in common. Mulya and his wife, Nadya—also an old friend from their high school Moscow gang—had quickly found cheap tickets and an inexpensive hotel in Nice, left their kids with *dacha*-owning grandparents, and met Yasha for a week-long reunion on the Riviera. Jake was able to switch the return date of the vacation he had planned with Erin to five days earlier, which ended up putting him in Amsterdam on the eve of Yom Kippur.

JAKE MUST HAVE SWITCHED PLANES at Schiphol a couple dozen times but had never stayed in Amsterdam before. Here in Amsterdam, outside the central station littered with raggedy British and Australian youths, the air was dense with fog. All colors were dimmed. There were more bicycles than pedestrians in the streets. Seagulls circled around garbage bins. And yet there was something about this city that struck Jake right away as extremely livable and free-spirited. As he walked slowly to his hotel-boat anchored on the Amstel, he kept bumping into the signs of an old city culture. He observed to himself that the citizens of Amsterdam looked bourgeois, but not at all philistine. He also gladly noted and later wrote down in his journal that young Dutch women in the afternoon crowd returned his inquisitive looks with a sensual readiness that revealed no fear of a stranger. What a beautiful place for a Jew to atone, Jake thought to himself and smiled.

After checking into his hotel-boat, Jake went to a cozy, glass-enclosed restaurant on Damrak and gorged on a delightfully unhealthy veal cutlet with thick slabs of fried potatoes. It was four o'clock, and he decided to start fasting at six-thirty. That left him with more than two hours to sort out his many thoughts in anticipation of the annual Day of Atonement.

So it's Yom Kippur, Jake told himself, finishing a second beer. Have I sinned? Was breaking up with Erin a sin? Or was it a mitzvah? How can I atone if I haven't sinned? Am I a Jew only because I couldn't, wouldn't marry Erin? Jake knew he wasn't thinking straight after the sleepless night he had spent partying and parting with his Russian friends in Nice, the early morning flight, and the beer he had drunk since having arrived in Amsterdam. He knew he wasn't aiming his mind in the right direction, but couldn't help it. What he wanted from this nearing Yom Kippur were some real answers. He began to blame himself for ending it with Erin so abruptly. I should've taken it slower, given her more time to come to grips with my reasons. The foggy air outside the restaurant changed color from blue to putty. Jake asked for a cup of coffee. Maybe I should've simply married her—and to hell with the whole Jewish thing. He remembered his first dinner date with Erin, in a seafood place in

Baltimore's Inner Harbor. She didn't sleep with him for an entire month, and he almost didn't mind the deferring of sex, so much did she make him relish the prolonged foreplay. Jake suddenly felt all alone in the city of Amsterdam, craving a woman's company. He summoned the bulbous waiter and, acting a lot more drunk, asked, "Where is your vicious red light district? I've gotta check it out!"

Not one bit surprised, the waiter came back with a pocket map of central Amsterdam, resembling a page from the atlas of human anatomy: blue veins of canals, black nerves of main streets, red muscles of bridges.

"Cross Damrak and go straight. You can't miss it." The waiter bowed, accepting Jake's payment and tip.

Some incomprehensible magnetism navigated Jake's body through an evening crowd on main streets, then down a long deserted alley laid with cobblestones. A few minutes later he found himself strolling along a narrow, seedy canal in the company of other men, walking by themselves or in groups of two or three. A couple would occasionally flit by; Jake even spotted a family of tourists with two children, a boy and a girl dressed in yellow rain jackets. Some visitors took pictures, flashes from their cameras sinking to the bottom of the canal. On both sides of the canal stood Gothic-looking buildings, murky and narrow. Each had several glass doors. Jake was initially embarrassed to peer closely at those doors. He walked back and forth for a while, observing what seemed to be a nightly routine in this extraordinary neighborhood. He had read and heard about Amsterdam's red light district, but never imagined it to be so peaceful, so devoid of the filth and crime that he would attribute to such areas in most other cities. Some of the glass doors had screens or blinds, and burgundy red lanterns shone from behind the doors—an indication that the hostess was busy with a customer. It was chilly and dank out, so only occasionally did he see an open door and a woman in lacy lingerie standing in the doorway. For the most part, the women stood behind closed glass doors, smiling and waving, enticing the visitors.

Streetlamps alongside the canal gave out yellow gassy light. Framed by the glass doors, the women's figures looked like fading old portraits. Jake identified the local business code: a light tap, the door half opens, bargaining if any, the curtain falls, and the red magic lantern comes alight, visible through the chinks in the blinds.

He could make out his own reflection on the canal: a large meaty chin, reddish stubble, aquiline nose, thick curly eyebrows, deep-set brown eyes. He finally made his choice. The brass knob looked like it had just been polished. A good omen, Jake said to himself. He leaned against the door, licking his dry lips and wiping his perspiring forehead with a white handkerchief. Inside, from beyond the glass, a blonde woman in her midtwenties studied her next customer. She then pursed her thin lips and unlocked the door.

"Come upstairs, it's chilly down here. I've turned the heat up."

The prostitute spoke clean English with just a residue of a Germanic accent that dulled her consonants. She wore white silk panties and a bra adorned with oxblood lace. Jake watched her ascend the stairs like a slinky Siamese cat. She had slim hips and a small, boyish behind. Her breasts were ample for her height and figure, and her hair was dyed.

"It's seventy guilders for a fuck or a suck. You pay first."

Jake was amazed by the sheer automatism with which this pale face commanded him. He opened his wallet and paid. The woman stashed the money away, rolled down her underwear, then undid her bra and laid it out carefully on a wooden chair. The room was lit by four large red candles, each burning in a corner. The bed was narrow and covered with an Oriental bedspread. A glass-topped coffee table. Two chairs. Bare painted walls. A mirror mounted on the ceiling above the bed. Jake stepped in place, unsure of what was next.

"What are you waiting for? You can take your clothes off."

Jake blushed to the roots of his hair.

"May I have some water? My mouth is very dry." He sounded like a teenager buying cigarettes.

"I don't usually do that for customers, but I'll make an exception for you. Please don't break the cup." The prostitute filled a blue porcelain cup with tap water. "It's a gift."

Jake greedily gulped the water down.

"Water tastes good here. Thank you."

He was now sitting on the edge of the bed, she—in the chair directly across, having a smoke.

"Listen, I don't quite know how to tell you this," Jake interrupted the silence. "I don't really want to have sex. I'm feeling kind of lonely. Do you think we could just talk for a while?"

"I knew you were one of *those* from the way you stared. It's the same if we talk or fuck, as long as the money keeps coming. If you want to stay for thirty minutes, that would be a hundred guilders more."

"That's pretty steep," Jake took out his wallet again and counted the foreign bills twice.

The prostitute put on a purple sweatshirt and set an alarm clock.

"What's your name?" Jake asked, now feeling more at ease with his hostess.

"It's Annette."

"You're Dutch?"

"No, German, from Hamburg."

"What brings you to Amsterdam? Sorry, dumb question, I take it back." Jake shrugged his shoulders, which was his way of showing regret.

"And what brings you to Amsterdam?" Annette retorted.

Jake's first instinct was to tell her about Erin, his trip to Nice, and about spending Yom Kippur in Amsterdam. But something stopped him.

"I'm doing a piece on tourism in this city. I'm a writer." Jake was surprised by the way this almost-lie came out.

"It seems that half of my clients are writers. Can't you come up with a better lie?"

"Actually—"

"It's not my business," the prostitute interrupted him. "You're Jewish, aren't you?" she said and looked him straight in the eyes.

"How did you know?"

"You look Jewish."

"How can you tell? Back in the States very few can."

"My father was Jewish. You have the same sadness in your eyes, even when you smile. My father used to say it came from many centuries of being outcasts."

"Is your mother German?"

"Yes. She and my dad are circus gymnasts. I used to perform until age seventeen."

"I want to ask you something, Annette. How can you do this?"

"Do what?" she lit another cigarette and parted her legs.

"Well, this, I mean, doesn't it bother you that you sleep with all sorts of strange men for money? Please don't get me wrong, I am not a moralist, but still."

"What's there to understand? It's a job. The money's good. Living is cheaper in Amsterdam. I'm saving a lot."

"What are you going to do with it?"

"First of all, I'd like to buy a nice apartment in the south of France. There's a lot I want."

The alarm went off, sounding like a firemen's siren. Jake got up and put on his long raincoat.

"Well, many thanks for your time." He stopped in the middle of the room and wanted to shake her hand.

"I don't shake hands with men at work. No offense." She smiled for the first time.

"Well, then, let me ask you one last question."

"Okay, but make it short."

"Did your parents have a good marriage? I mean did it matter to them that one was Jewish and the other wasn't?"

"I'm afraid you will have to come again if you want to know more. Plus, I'm not sure I wish to talk about it. Just remember: difference is only good when you can comprehend it."

Annette opened the door and turned the staircase lights on. "Don't forget your umbrella. It's pouring outside."

She was right; squalls of rain washed over the cobblestones, filling the canals with autumn quicksilver.

THE NEXT MORNING Jake slept until ten o'clock. Waking up in a narrow bed in his second-class cabin, trying to toss his body back into sleep, he felt the first calls of hunger. He had to hold out until evening. In an outdoor café with wet chairs, Jake asked for a cup of tea with lemon; on Yom Kippur he always allowed himself to drink tea with lemon but without sugar. The young waitress had bright copper hair. She offered him a piece of freshly baked apple cake.

"Honestly, I'd love to, but I can't. I have to fast today."

"I see," the waitress smiled sympathetically.

A Baedeker map in hand, Jake headed south, first down Rokin, then along Vijzelstraat. He traversed half-a-dozen canals, stopping to examine the old railings and reliefs. His eyes spotted now a baby lion, now a cupid, now a dragon. He turned right onto Wetering and soon found himself facing the Rijksmuseum square. He went inside the massive arch where street painters offered their wares and a band of four jazzmen played Glen Miller. From Gleb, a beared artist from St. Petersburg, he bought a tiny framed lithograph: a houseboat resembling Jake's hotel, a bridge casting a convex shadow, and a stray bicycle.

Jake liked it in Amsterdam; he liked the warm foggy air, the young mothers pushing their strollers, the maple leaves gyrating on the surface of the canals. He felt wanted and accepted here, wanted by the elderly gentleman, probably a banker, whom he asked for directions to the Film Museum; wanted by the two shop assistants at a shoe store where he ended up buying a pair of black rubber soles. He liked his unprescribed way of atoning in the streets of Amsterdam, his head more and more transparent with hunger, his body ready to levitate. Around four it started raining again, first a drizzle, then a downpour, and he went back to the hotel to change into good clothes.

I could be happy here, he said to himself while walking back. I could really be happy here just being nobody, a man in the crowd, a scarlet maple leaf traveling to the sea down one of the waterways.

Having left his umbrella at the hotel, he was soon completely soaked, feeling like Jonah in the whale's wet womb. "Bridge, bicycle, behemoth, baritone, Bilderdijkstraat, burgomaster"—under his breath Jake gibbered a variation on his day's impressions and Old Testament heroic narratives. "Can you lift a behemoth from the swamp, ha, can you? Can you marry a non-Jewish girl? How's that for a question?"

Jake showered, dried himself off, and, wrapped only in a towel from the waist down, made an entry in his journal. He then put on his clothes, including a tie and jacket, examined himself in the mirror, pulled a raincoat on, and went out into the downpour. He headed east, to the old Portuguese synagogue in the former Jewish quarter. "The Sephardic synagogue," Jake remembered his father's dear crowing voice at the end of the line, "was built in the seventeenth century. It is one of the grandest synagogues in the entire world. You must visit it, son." His father went on and on about the proud Sephardic Jews of Amsterdam, about the way the synagogue's courtyard was supposed to resemble the Temple of Solomon.

Now, plowing through the rain, Jake tried to picture in his head the building where he was to hear that year's shofar. Probably because of the associations with Sephardic Jews, he envisioned a Moorish-style building. The synagogue was marked on his map, he knew the exact address, L. E. Visserplein, corner of Muiderstraat, but what he saw did not look at all like what he had expected. It was a cubic form made of dark brick, with a balustrade all but hiding the roof from view. Taller than any of its neighbors, the massive structure reminded Jake of an old bank or an armory or a mint. He walked around it, found the main entrance, and tried to open the heavy door, above which a stone pelican was feeding three young birds. It was locked. He knocked. No answer. What the hell is going on? How can a shul not be open on Yom Kippur? he thought as he banged at the door. This must be a different building—and the architecture isn't Moorish, Jake reasoned with himself. He walked a few hundred yards, hoping to ask for directions, but there was no one in sight. He found himself in a neighborhood of brownstones with high porches, white columns, and porticoes. As he turned to head back to the main street, a door opened, and two women and a girl of five or six walked out into the rain. Walking slowly and proudly in the direction from which he had just come, the three of them looked perfectly middle-class Dutch to Jake, with their light hair, pale skin, and solid, respectable clothes. But when he peered closer, one thing seemed odd: all three, even the little girl, wore long wool skirts. The women's hats had black veils. Are they going to a funeral? On Thursday night and at this hour? Jake wondered as he followed the procession of three long skirts. They brought him back to the dark cubic building with high windows and a bal-ustrade. One of the women knocked at the main door, but there was no answer. The three waited for a few minutes, musing, then Jake heard a long squeaky sound. A gate opened on the side of the building, and a male voice said something in Dutch. Jake rushed to the gate and peeked inside. He saw several athletically built men with dark beards and curly hair, in yarmulkes, smoking and quietly conversing. He came in and addressed one of the "guards," as he immediately labeled them.

"Shalom, excuse me, can I get inside the shul?"

"Shalom, my friend, you must be American," replied one of the guards, offering Jake a plain black skullcap.

"Thanks, I brought mine," Jake said, reaching for his pocket.

The squeaky gate was locked, and Jake heard the clanking of a heavy latch. He walked up several white steps and saw two doors, on the left and on the right. "The right one must be for the women's gallery," Jake thought. He entered a huge sanctuary. Diffuse light fell in through bow-shaped windows. The cubic space was divided into three aisles. Rows of marble columns supported the vaulting of the roof. There were additional smaller columns laid out against the walls. Separate half-columns supported the upstairs gallery. Jake liked the arrangement of seats downstairs: brackets of dark wooden benches placed opposite each other on either side of the space. This way, men in the congregation faced each other as they prayed. The Holy Ark was in the far wall, the elevated rostrum opposite it stood in the near end of the room. Jake sat in the corner of a bench and began eyeing the congregation. It was about five in the evening, and there were altogether about two hundred people. The sanctuary gradually fell into semidarkness, the windows changing color from blue-gray to smokey gray to the color of an overcast night sky. More and more people arrived the closer it came to the blowing of the shofar. Two hours later the synagogue was nearly full.

Jake didn't care to follow the service; he knew little Hebrew and on High Holy Days at home went to Reform services. Instead, he was preoccupied with studying the members of the congregation, men and boys. He could distinguish two types of faces. One was angular, olive-skinned, distinctly Mediterranean. Those men for the most part were thickset and not very tall; their eyes were dark, their distinct noses crooked, their hair black or occasionally reddish. They were the descendants of the Sephardic Jews from Portugal and Spain, the founders of this Amsterdam community. Beside them, outnumbering the Sephardic faces, sat what looked to Jake like typical Dutchmen or northern Germans. These men were tall and had fair skin, light hair, and oblong faces with small, sharp noses. "These are the Ashkenazim; they have some German, Polish, and Lithuanian genes," Jake imagined his father saying.

Among the men of the congregation Jake found four especially intriguing. One looked like Mr. Pickwick: fat, with pudgy cheeks and a triple chin, a gentle smile and bulging, humor-filled eyes. Along with about thirty other men in the congregation, including the cantor, "Mr. Pickwick" was dressed in tails and a top hat. Then there was a grim Jew with an impressive nose and a spade-shaped beard. He had two teenage boys with him, both with Negroid features and premature black shadows on their upper lips. With the tassels of their prayer shawls they were tickling the neck of a boy who was praying in the next row. Jake also observed a tall, slender gentleman, a lawyer or a financier, he conjectured, very calm, very sure of himself, with cold green eyes and reading spectacles on the tip of his pointed nose. Finally, there was an old Jew in a three-piece navy suit shiny with age and wear, who prayed zealously; his face was bristly, his back was hunched, and his large pink ears jutted out.

The cantor came up to the rostrum. He looked like a retired infantry colonel, with short silvery hair, a neatly trimmed, small mustache, and a square jaw. In contrast to his severe appearance, his voice was soft and enveloping. "Oh it melts butter, it really melts butter," Jake recalled his mother's excitement after hearing Richard Tucker in *La Bohéme* at the Met. While the cantor sang, the temple became completely dark, inviting the night in. Only the rostrum remained well lit. Two men went around the walls and columns, lighting candles. They moved quietly and slowly so as not to disturb the cantor and congregation now joined in the mystery of atonement. The temple gradually began to glow with hundreds of flames.

Candlelight and guttural singing focused Jake's thoughts and lifted him from a wearing-on drowsiness. Although he didn't feel alien to this tightly knit congregation, he still felt alone. Besides, the absence of women on the floor made him think of the wives of all the praying men. Were they upstairs preparing to reunite with their husbands and sons? *Every Jew shall marry and have a wife,* ran through Jake's mind. Here he was, thirty-six and nowhere near marriage. Erin came to his mind, along with the two years of what he used to think was happiness. Then their sudden separation. *How can we love someone and not stay with that person?* he thought, now rocking and swaying to the cantor's chant. With his eyes closed and his fingers interlocked, he revisited in his mind some of the places he had gone together with Erin. Annapolis, their regular haunt. Key West in March. The Sun Valley for skiing. Then he recalled that village in the mountains of northern Vermont where they had spent a week during their first summer together.

The edges of the meadow had glittered with wild strawberries. Tired of picking with their hands, they had crawled on their knees, eating the small devilishly sweet berries right off the stems. They were all alone on their meadow. Fringes of mountains, some shadowed, some lit by the ripening sun. Humming of bees. Gradually they had moved to the far side of the meadow, away from a dirt road. They were lying in the shade underneath rustling trees—Jake in a pair of denim shorts, Erin in a tank-top and faded cotton leggings.

"Jake, do you know what I'm thinking?" Erin touched his chest.

"Tell me."

"This is how I want our life to be: a long meadow with wild strawberries."

"That would be nice. Long. And weekends without any work."

"Yes, and we would all go to church together, you, me, the kids."

Jake felt a cold hollow forming inside the chest. "Erin, you know that I don't go to church," he said dryly.

Dismay was scattered in Erin's eyes. Her cheeks turned scarlet.

"I mean . . . go somewhere spiritual as a family, not necessarily to church. Sweetums, what's wrong?"

"Nothing is wrong. Everything's fine."

She rolled over and kissed his stomach. Jake didn't stop her. Her right hand moved down his shorts. Then she brought her head down. As he slipped closer and closer to the boundary of life and that other, bodiless realm, he lifted up his head. Letting his eyes take in the far mountains, he shut them and did not open them until afterwards. He stared at the cloudless blue sky over his head. He felt with such intensity and verity that as his body had remained lying on the warm grass alongside his girlfriend's, some other part of him—the soul? the spirit? the breath?—had separated and flung itself to the zenith of the sky. He knew that Erin needed his words and caresses, but he couldn't find anything within him to offer her.

He had felt utterly alone at that moment. Then, right there, on that Vermont meadow, he had already known that something was amiss. Except that it took him another year to put that something into words.

The shrill sound of the shofar brought Jake back to Amsterdam. Looking around, he noticed two little girls in frilly dresses dash across one of the aisles. Laughing the jolliest of laughs, they ran up to the man Jake had earlier called "Mr. Pickwick." All Jake could make out in their prattle were "papa" and "shofar." Smiling with his watering eyes, the father of the little girls pressed a fat finger to his lips and then lifted them in turn and placed them on his lap. Both girls kissed their father and put their thin arms around his bulging neck. Didn't I already know back then in Vermont that I could never marry her? That I couldn't bear the thought of Sunday church with Erin and little boys or girls? Jake looked up at the vaulting dome of the temple, and a sudden joy of having atoned overcame him. Like the end of a long illness. A release. Members of the congregation greeted each other, some hugging and kissing, some shaking hands. Jake, too, shook hands with the men to his left and right, and hurried across the aisle toward the exit.

He found a restaurant around the corner from the Portuguese synagogue. Its interior resembled a ship's hold, with barrels used as tables. Jake ordered a double vodka, herring on toast, fish soup, and grilled liver with broccoli for the main course. "To your health," he smiled at the waitress. "Be always happy!" In a state nearing bliss, he swallowed all the food, left a large tip on the barrel, and went outside, inhaling the evening's briny moisture.

On the way back to his hotel-boat, Jake became aware of the piercing clarity with which he was seeing and remembering the buildings and objects he was passing and leaving behind: the charcoal silhouettes of the gable roofs, the moon gliding along and sliding down the wet luminous tiles, the shadows of barges gently swaying on the canals. A resplendence of being, a sensation of taking it all in. All of it was writing itself, coming to him in its completely revealed form. Jake was no longer thinking of Yom Kippur, of Erin, of Jewishness and Christianity. Those matters he had already understood, if not fully resolved in his heart, and this knowledge comforted him. He arrived at a plan—in the streets of Amsterdam: he would return to Baltimore, where after seventeen years his immigrant family had rooted themselves; they had even brought back from Moscow and reburied the remains of his father's parents. In four years, when Jake turned forty, he would have lived in America for half his life. Leaving Russia at nineteen, he had carried with him on the plane baggage so heavy that it took him years to unload it and so lofty that there were still times he couldn't stand solidly on American ground. That first flight over the Atlantic was also a flight from all the demons, monsters, and sirens a Jew can never seem to escape.

It had stopped raining, and Jake Glaz could smell the sweet mixture of leaves, of rotting leaves and gasoline and marijuana. As he stood on the lower deck of the hotel-boat, he gazed at flickering orange lights on the Amstel, and breathed the night of Amsterdam, and gently stroked it. He thought about tomorrow's flight back home to Baltimore, and with delight he pictured his American life that destiny held firm and tight and fondled in her deep blue pocket.